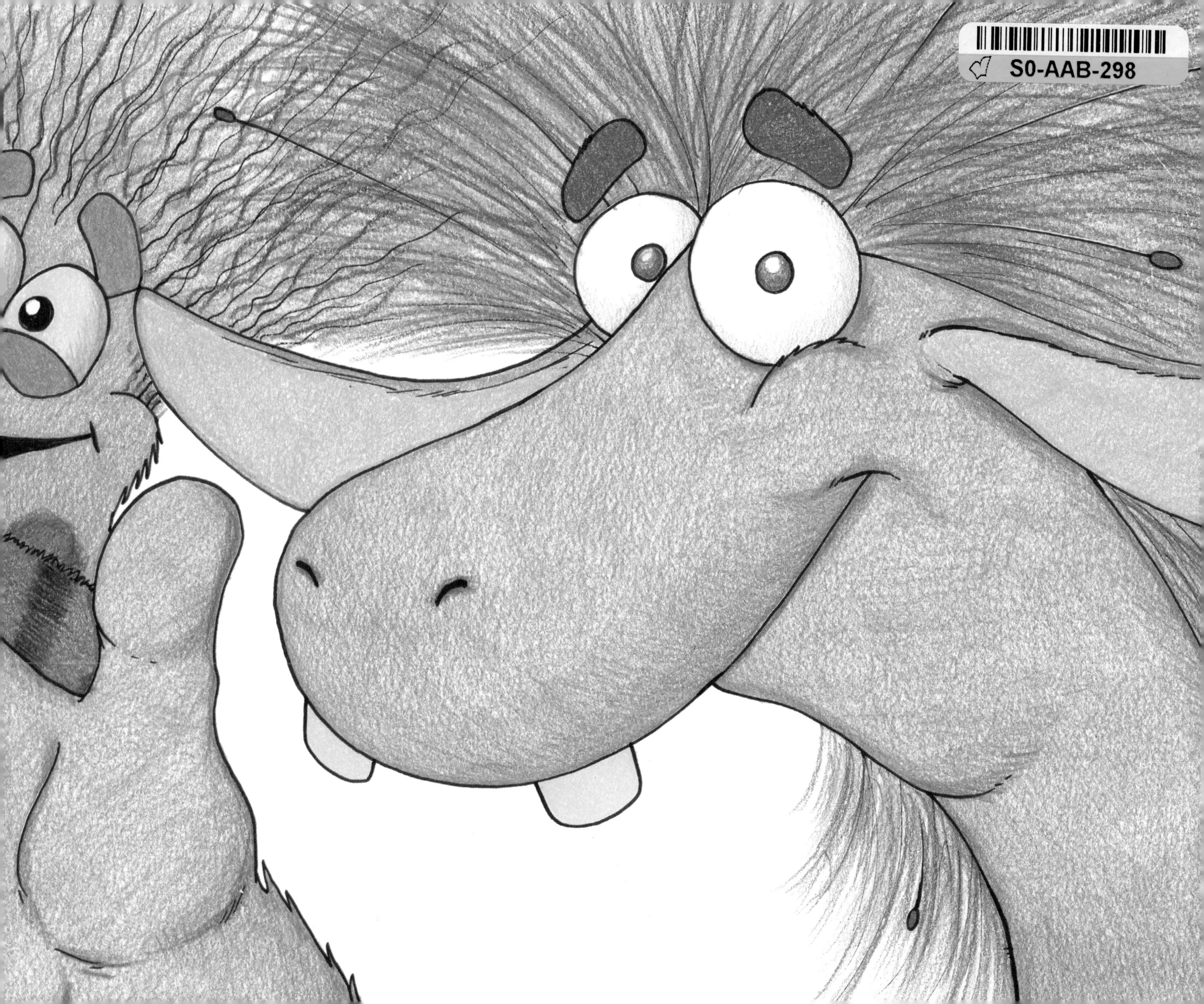

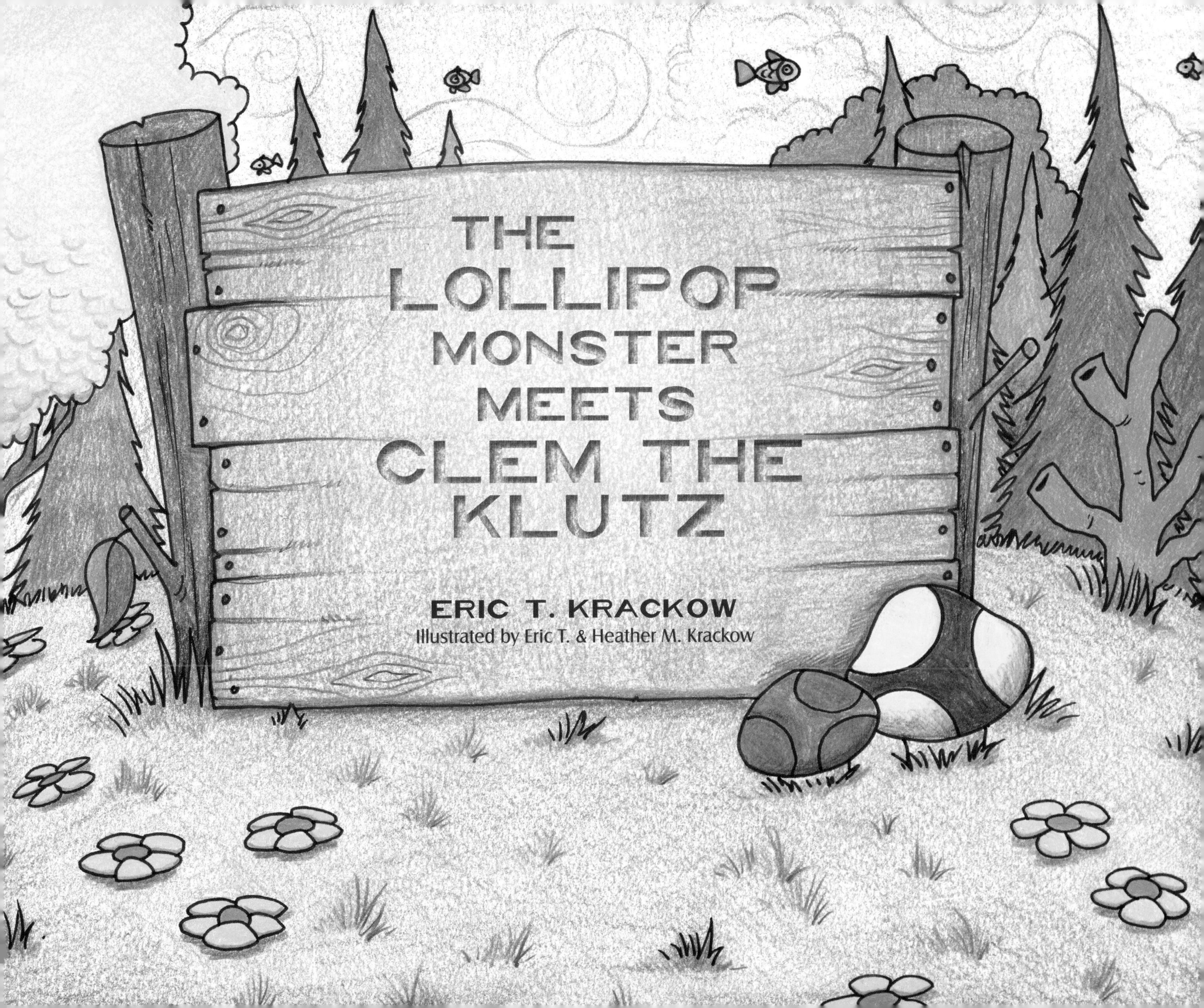

THE LOLLIPOP MONSTER MEETS CLEM THE KLUTZ

ERIC T. KRACKOW

Illustrated by Eric T. & Heather M. Krackow

OTHER SCHIFFER BOOKS BY THE AUTHOR:

The Lollipop Monster. ISBN: 978-0-7643-3773-4, $16.99,
Early reader — Ages 5-8

Bill the Snowman. ISBN: 978-0-7643-3219-7, $16.99,
Early reader — Ages 5-8

Have an Abominably Good Day. ISBN:978-0-7643-3496-2,
$16.99, Early reader — Ages 5-8

Copyright © 2013 by **ERIC T. KRACKOW**
Library of Congress Control Number: 2012955853

Designed by **DANIELLE D. FARMER**
Type set in Everyman/CastleT

ISBN: 978-0-7643-4287-5
Printed in China

Published by Schiffer Publishing, Ltd.
4880 Lower Valley Road
Atglen, PA 19310
Phone: (610) 593-1777; Fax: (610) 593-2002
E-mail: Info@schifferbooks.com

For the largest selection of fine reference books on this and related subjects, please visit our website at **www.schifferbooks.com.**

You may also write for a free catalog.
This book may be purchased from the publisher.
Please try your bookstore first.

We are always looking for people to write books on new and related subjects. If you have an idea for a book, please contact us at **proposals@schifferbooks.com**

Schiffer Books are available at special discounts for bulk purchases for sales promotions or premiums. Special editions, including personalized covers, corporate imprints, and excerpts can be created in large quantities for special needs. For more information contact the publisher.

In Europe, Schiffer books are distributed by
Bushwood Books
6 Marksbury Ave.
Kew Gardens
Surrey TW9 4JF England
Phone: 44 (0) 20 8392 8585; Fax: 44 (0) 20 8392 9876

This book is dedicated to
our two beautiful daughters

REBECCA
&
ANASTASIA

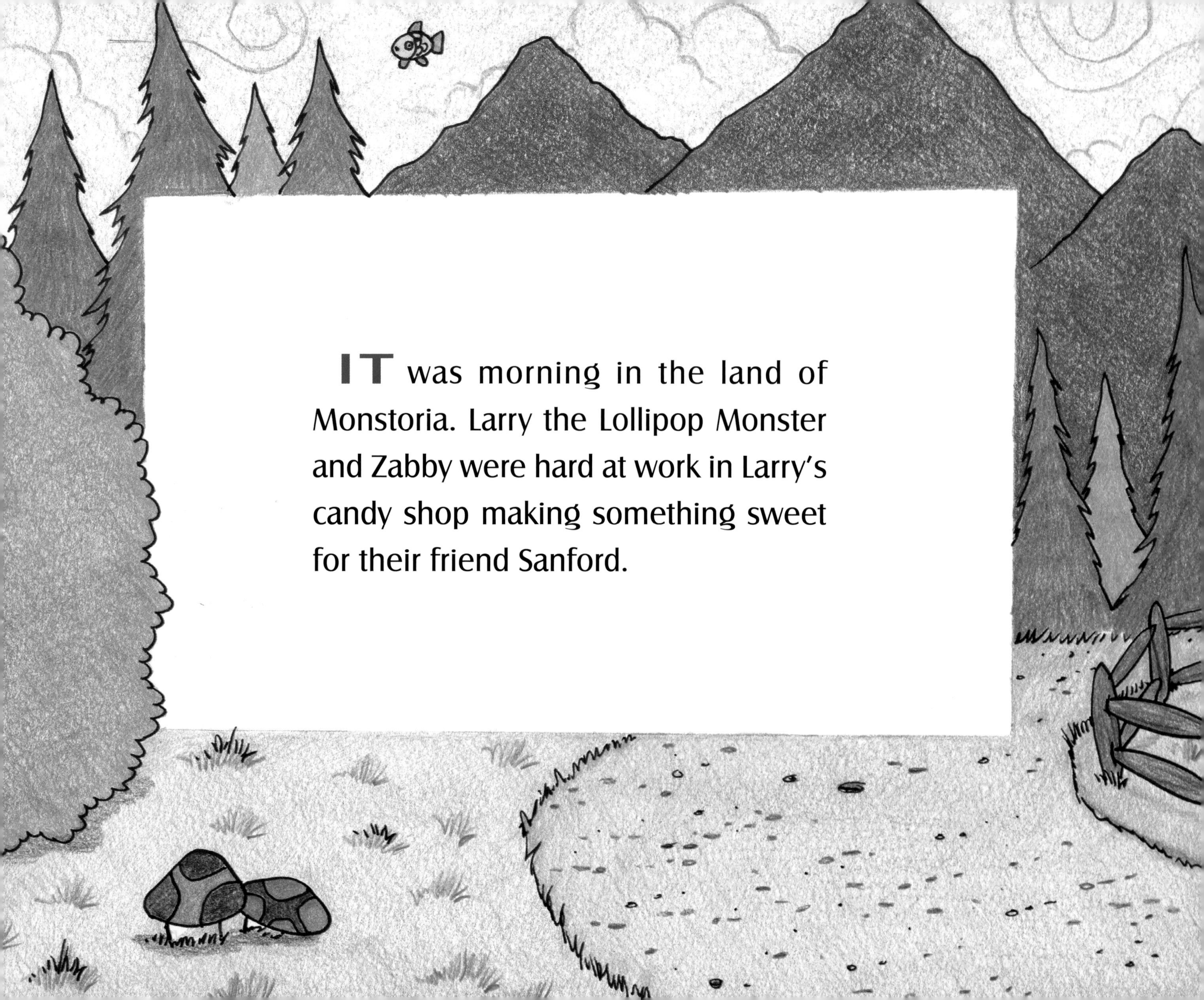

IT was morning in the land of Monstoria. Larry the Lollipop Monster and Zabby were hard at work in Larry's candy shop making something sweet for their friend Sanford.

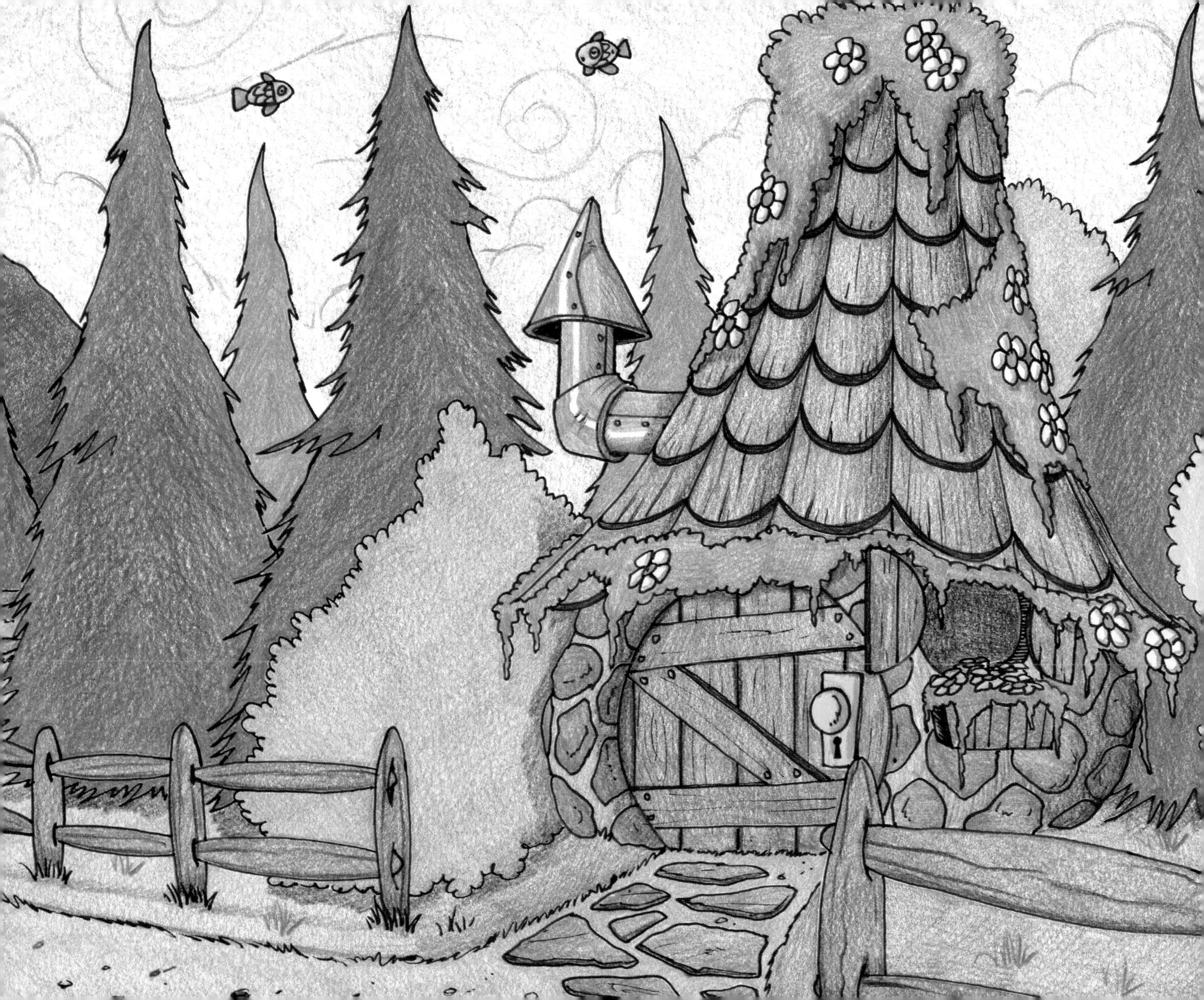

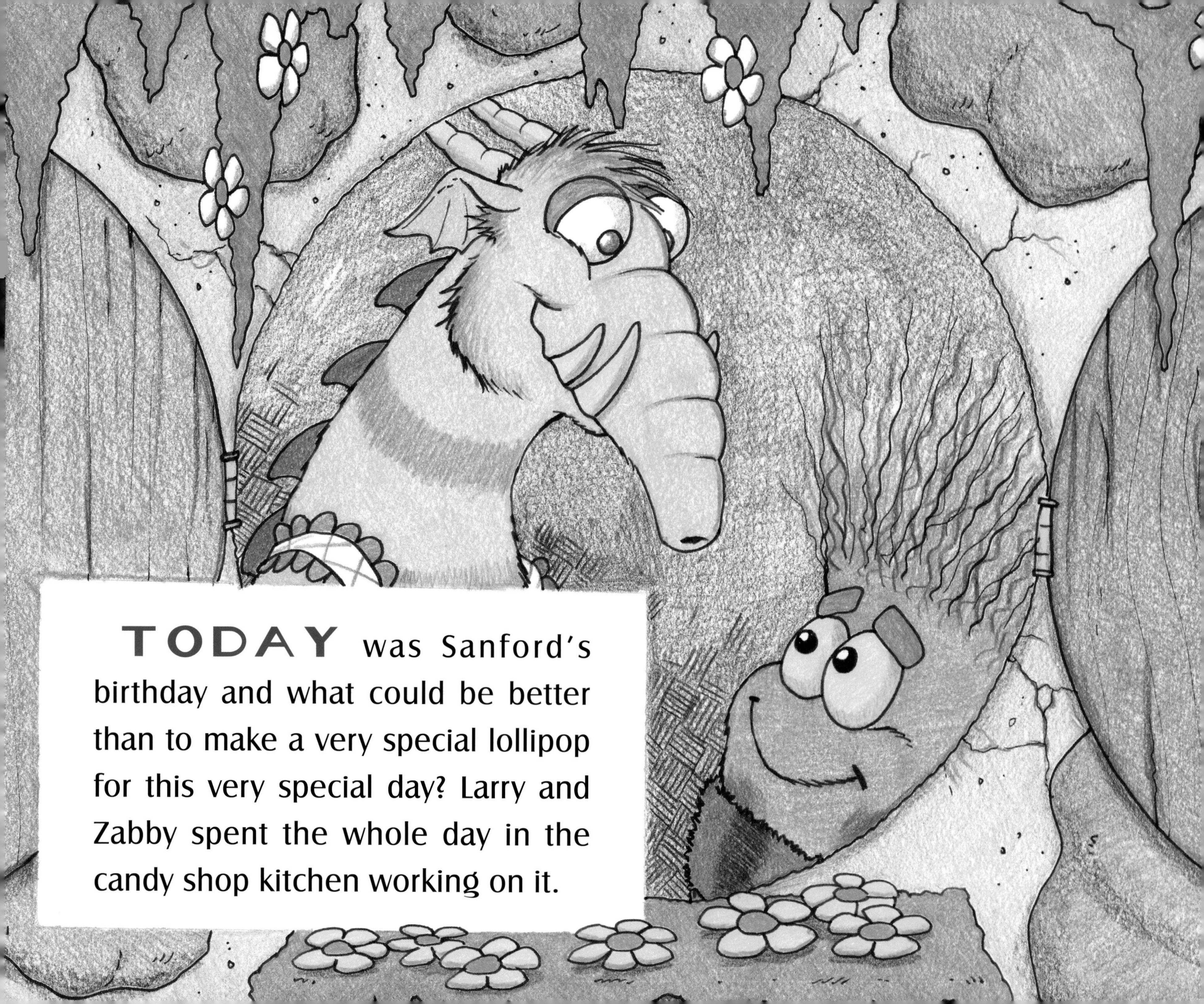

TODAY was Sanford's birthday and what could be better than to make a very special lollipop for this very special day? Larry and Zabby spent the whole day in the candy shop kitchen working on it.

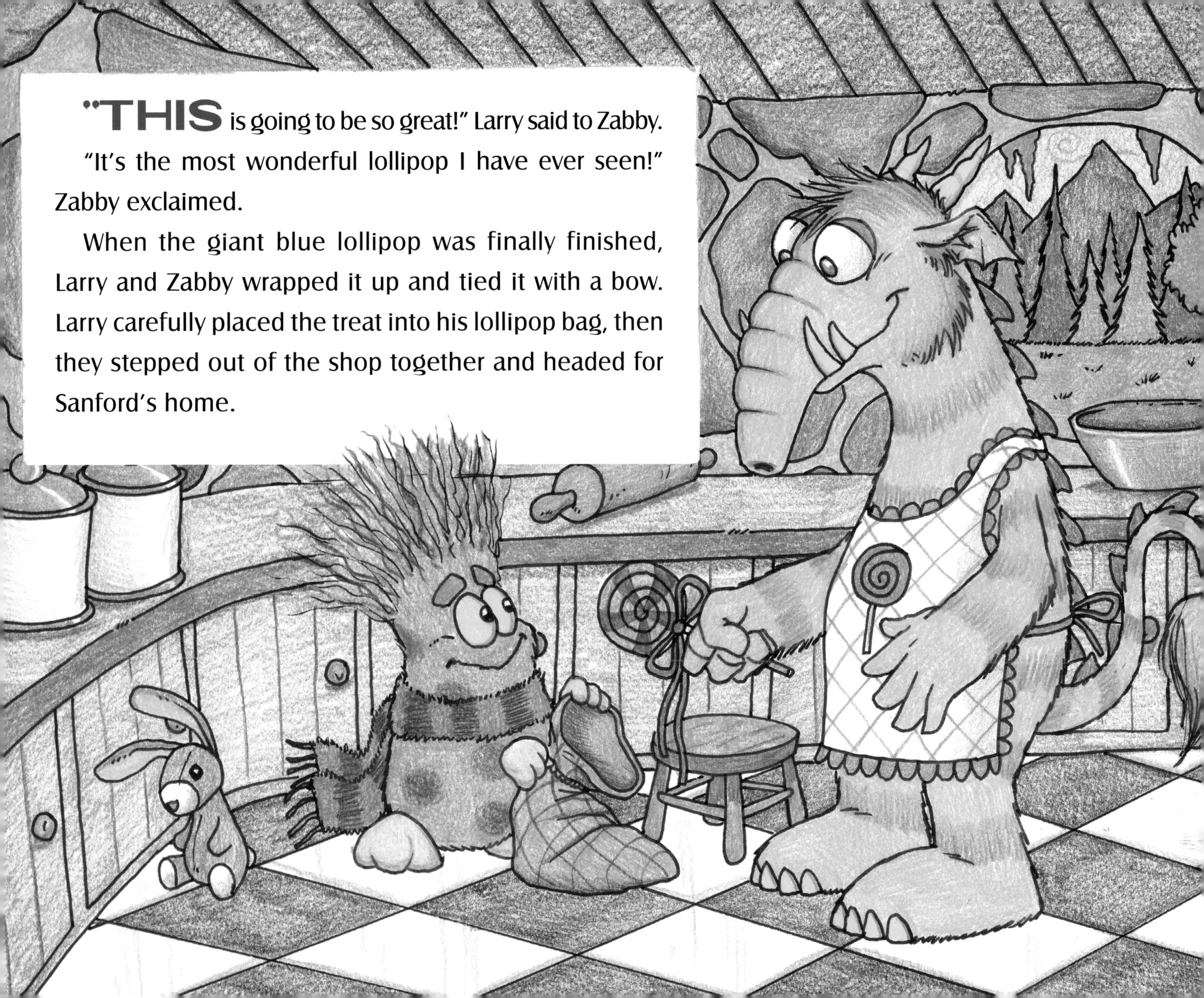

"THIS is going to be so great!" Larry said to Zabby.

"It's the most wonderful lollipop I have ever seen!" Zabby exclaimed.

When the giant blue lollipop was finally finished, Larry and Zabby wrapped it up and tied it with a bow. Larry carefully placed the treat into his lollipop bag, then they stepped out of the shop together and headed for Sanford's home.

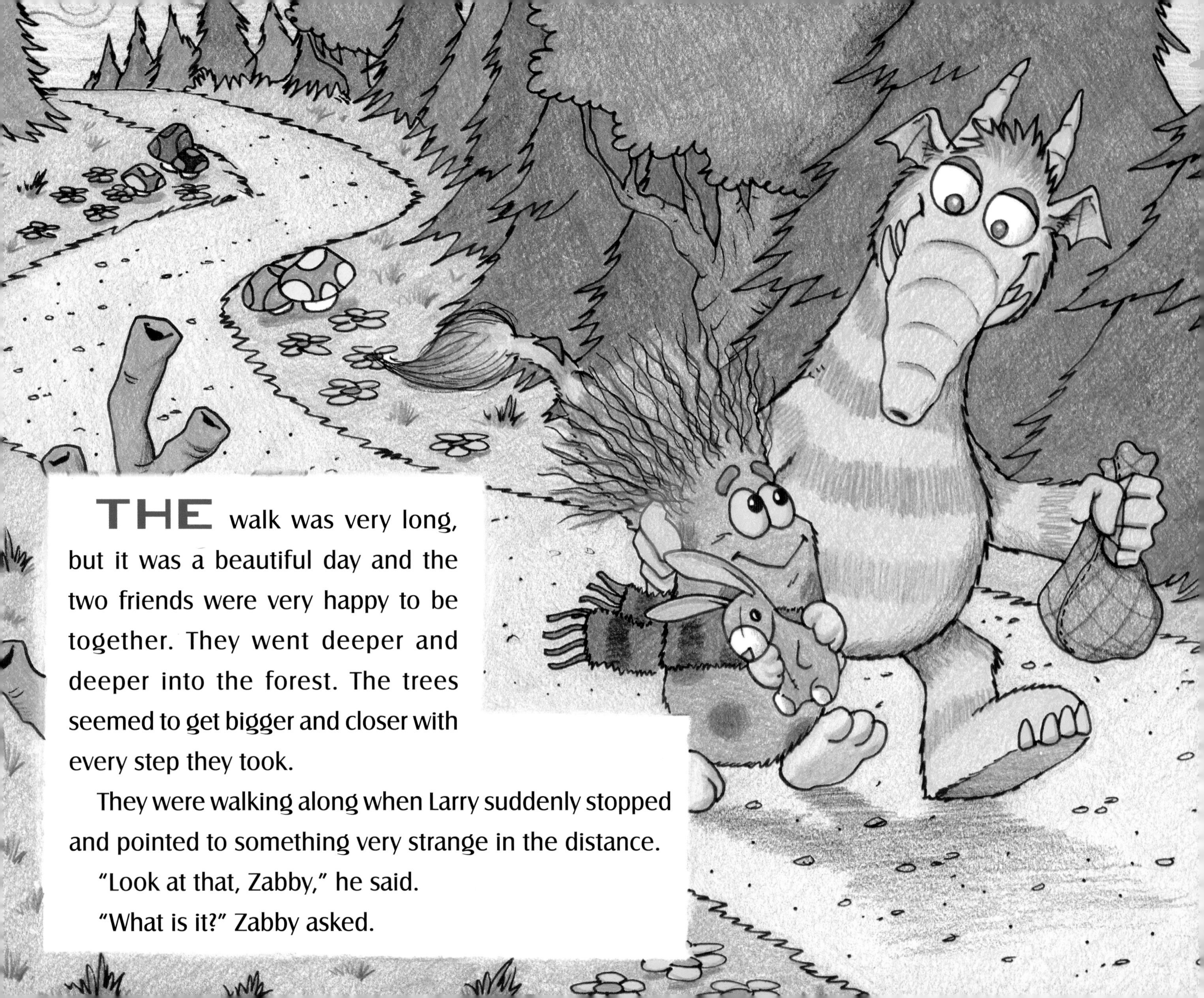

THE walk was very long, but it was a beautiful day and the two friends were very happy to be together. They went deeper and deeper into the forest. The trees seemed to get bigger and closer with every step they took.

They were walking along when Larry suddenly stopped and pointed to something very strange in the distance.

"Look at that, Zabby," he said.

"What is it?" Zabby asked.

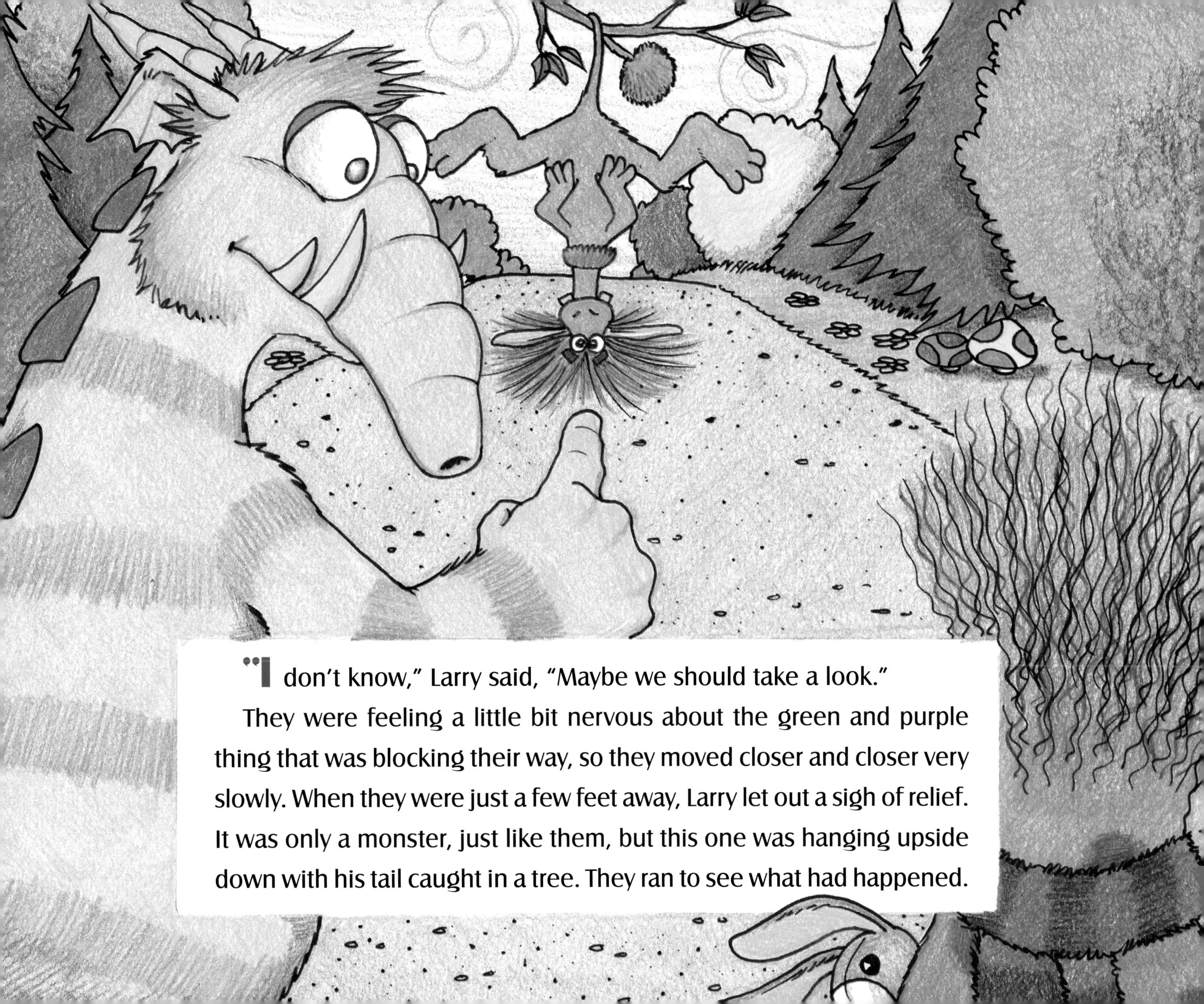

"I don't know," Larry said, "Maybe we should take a look."

They were feeling a little bit nervous about the green and purple thing that was blocking their way, so they moved closer and closer very slowly. When they were just a few feet away, Larry let out a sigh of relief. It was only a monster, just like them, but this one was hanging upside down with his tail caught in a tree. They ran to see what had happened.

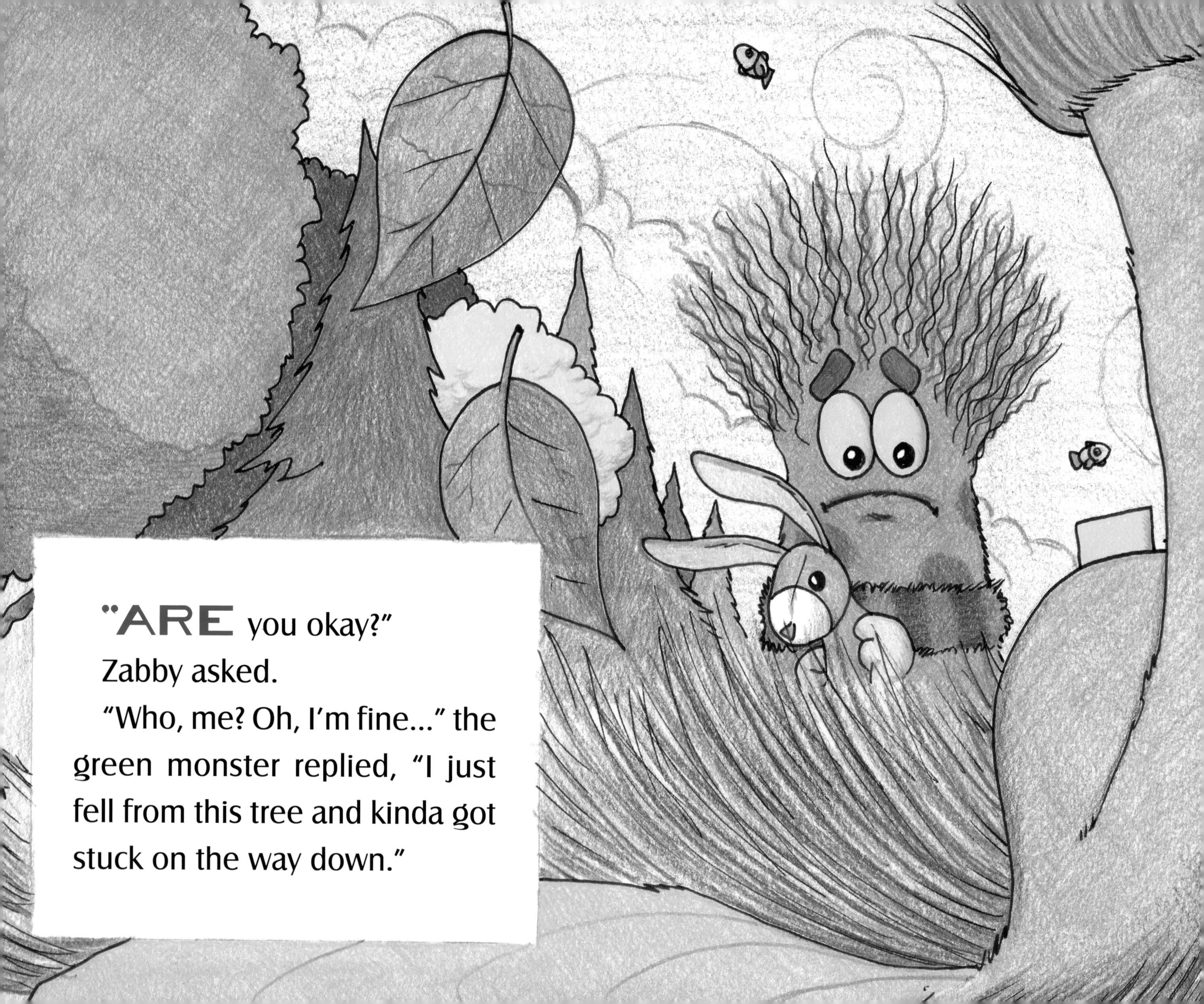

"ARE you okay?"

Zabby asked.

"Who, me? Oh, I'm fine…" the green monster replied, "I just fell from this tree and kinda got stuck on the way down."

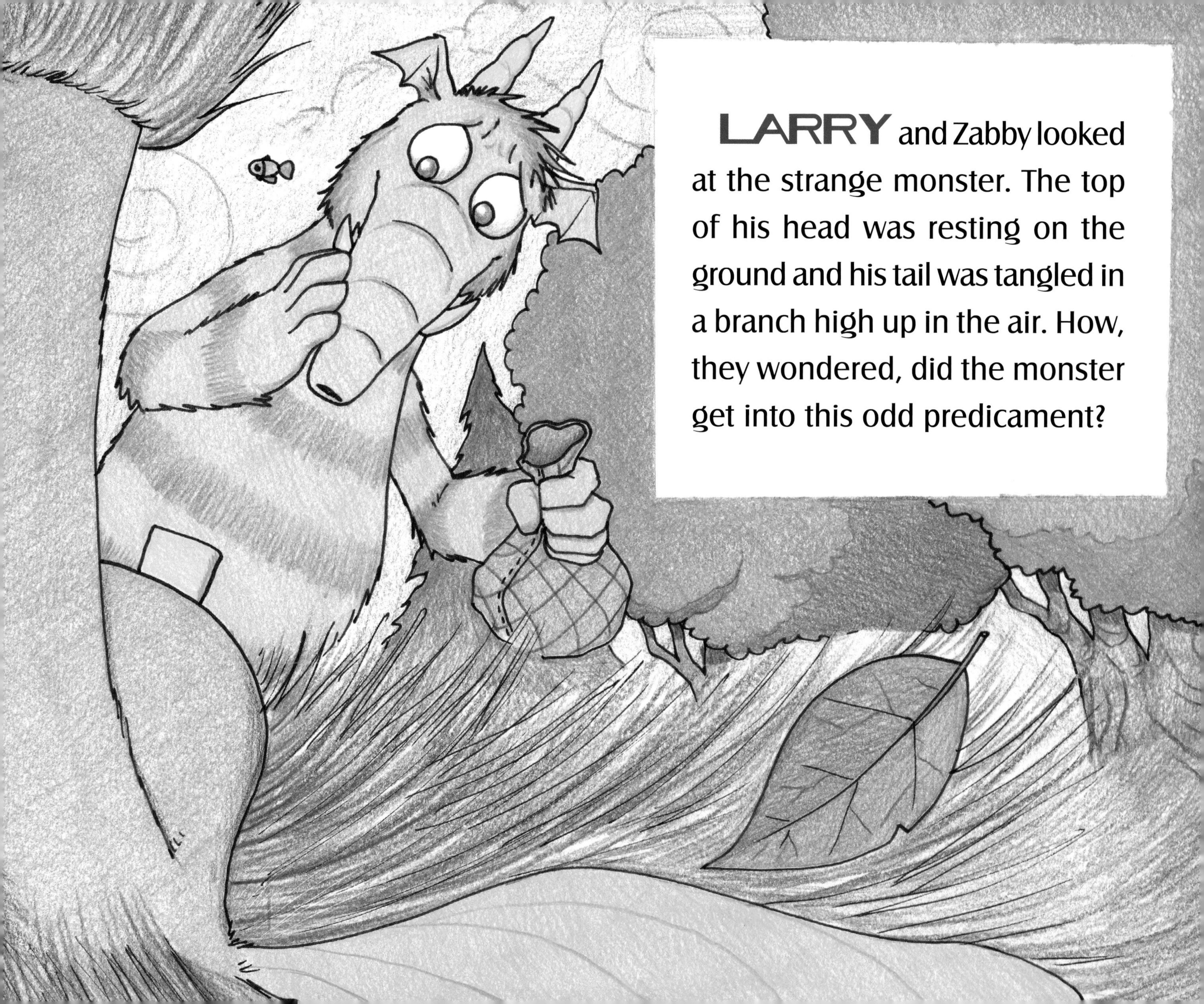

LARRY and Zabby looked at the strange monster. The top of his head was resting on the ground and his tail was tangled in a branch high up in the air. How, they wondered, did the monster get into this odd predicament?

LARRY then introduced himself to the silly monster. "My name is Larry and this is my very good friend, Zabby. What's your name?"

The upside down monster smiled and said, "My name is Clem, but some people call me Clem the Klutz."

"We're happy to meet you Clem," said Larry, "but you look like you could use some help."

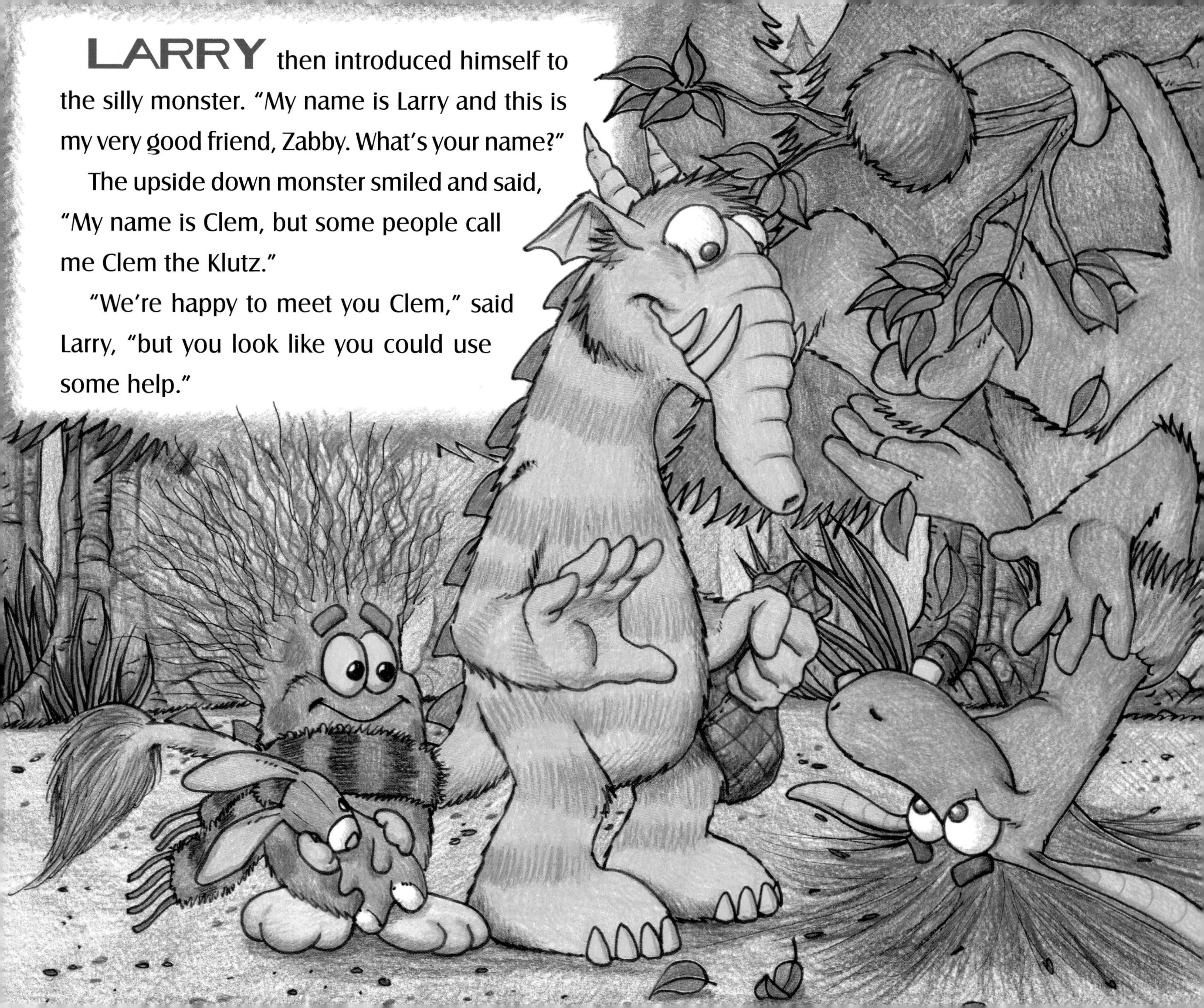

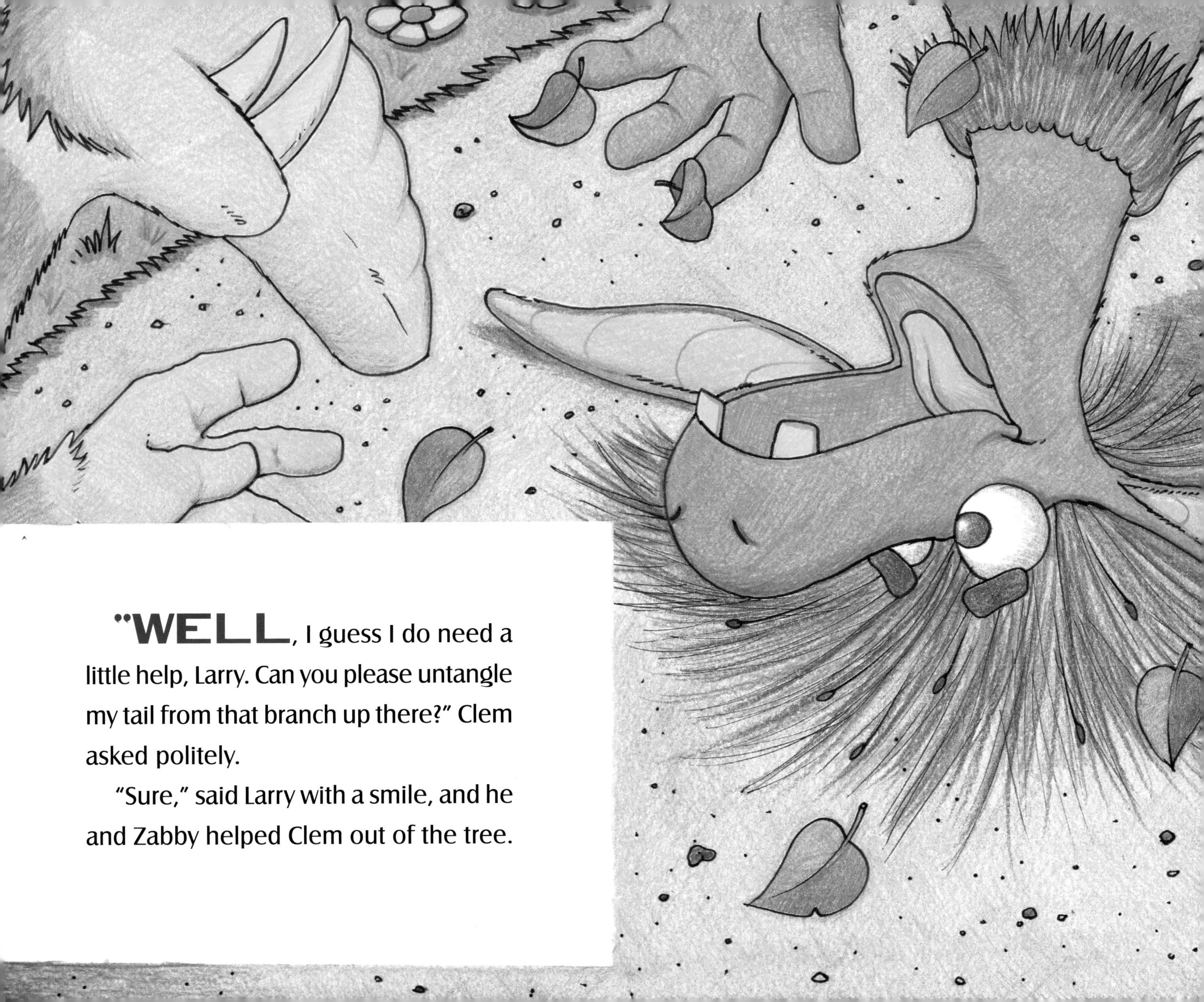

"**WELL**, I guess I do need a little help, Larry. Can you please untangle my tail from that branch up there?" Clem asked politely.

"Sure," said Larry with a smile, and he and Zabby helped Clem out of the tree.

"THANKS, Larry and Zabby," said Clem as he rubbed his sore neck, "I've been stuck there for quite some time!"

With Clem safely on the ground, Zabby couldn't wait to ask Clem the question that had been on their minds, "How in the world did you get stuck up there?"

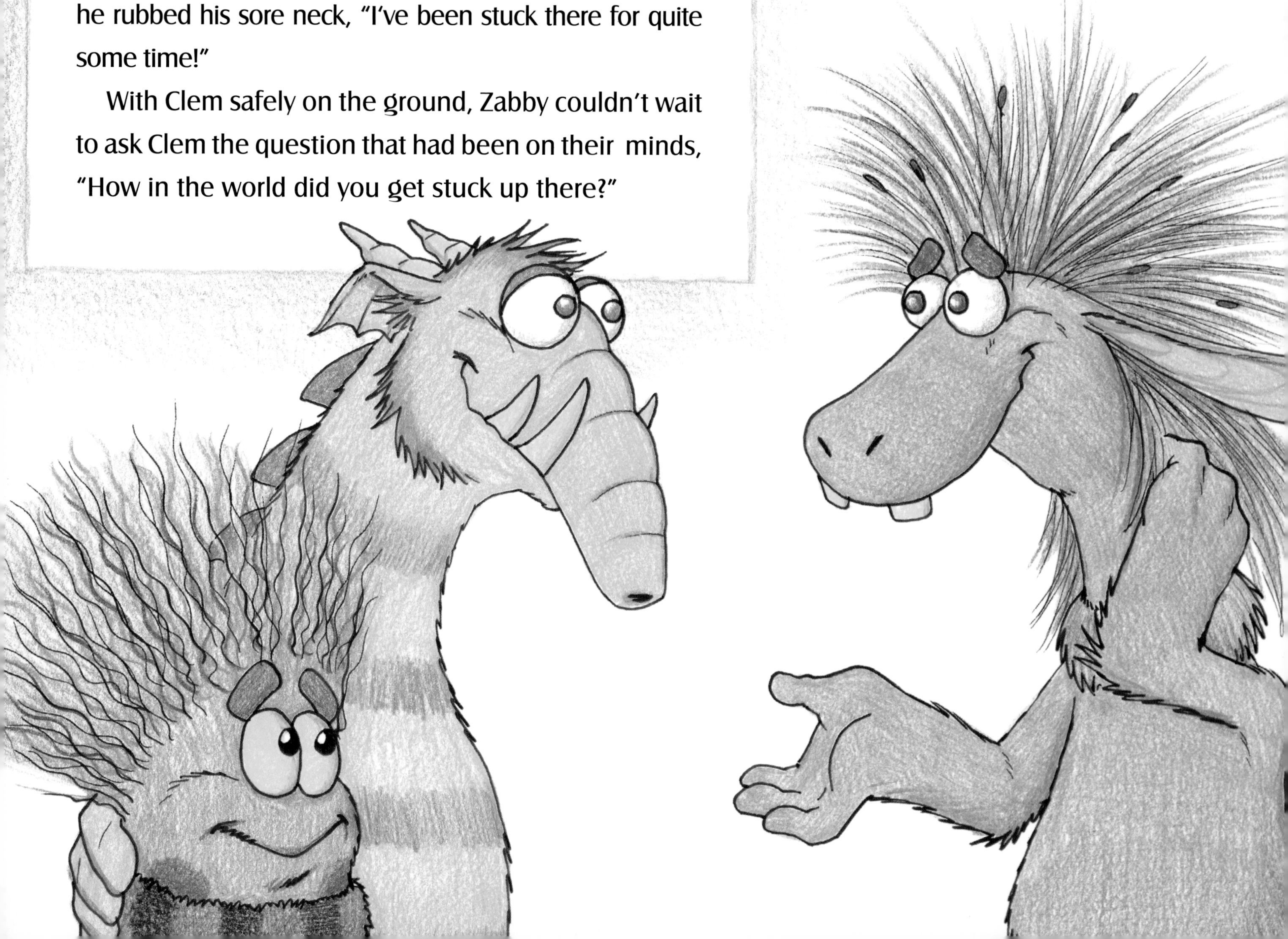

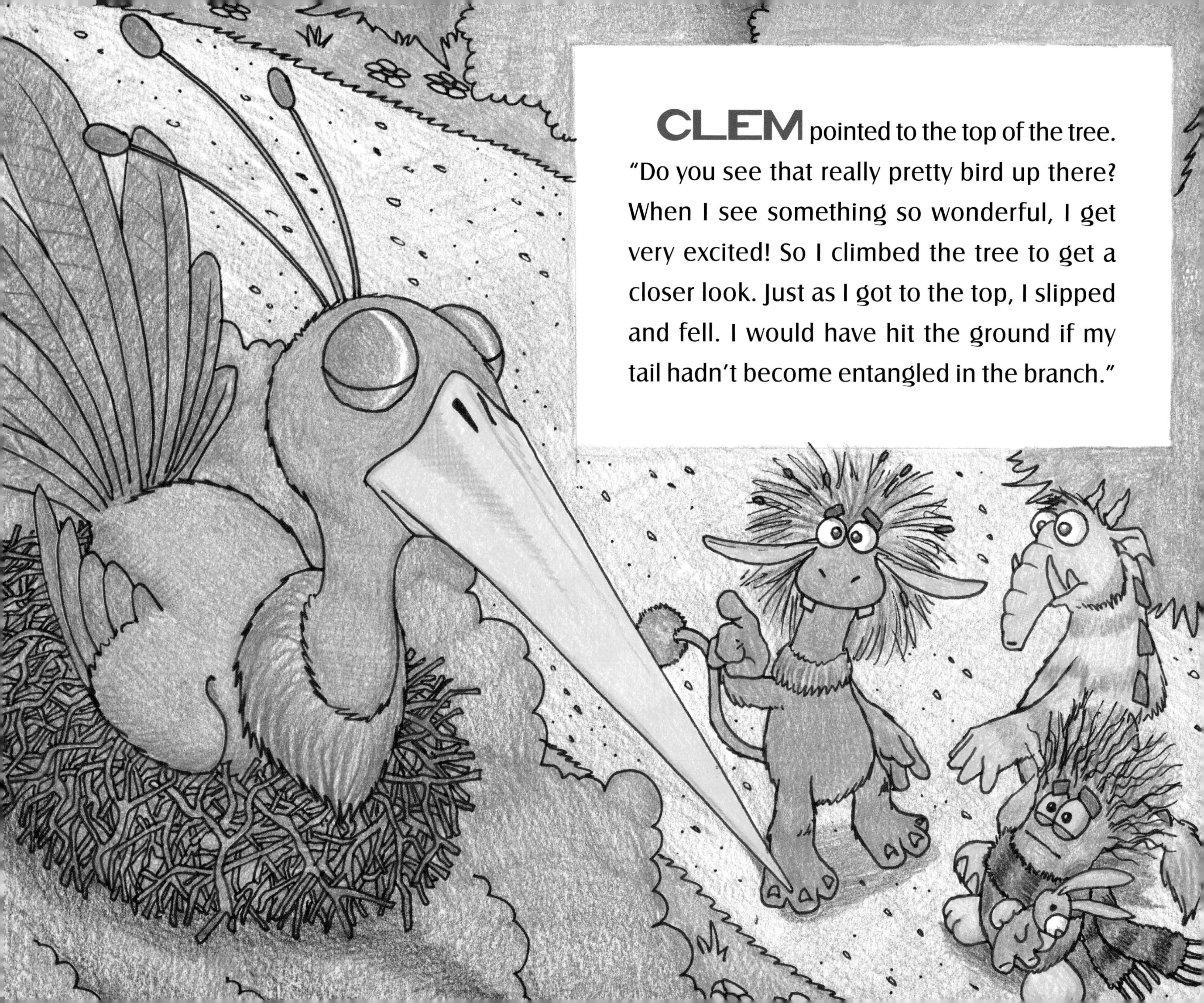

CLEM pointed to the top of the tree. "Do you see that really pretty bird up there? When I see something so wonderful, I get very excited! So I climbed the tree to get a closer look. Just as I got to the top, I slipped and fell. I would have hit the ground if my tail hadn't become entangled in the branch."

"**YOU** have had quite an adventure!" said Larry, "I'm sorry you didn't reach the bird, but I hope this will make you feel better." Larry reached into his bag and pulled out a yellow lollipop with orange swirls. Clem's eyes opened wide as Larry gave him the tasty treat.

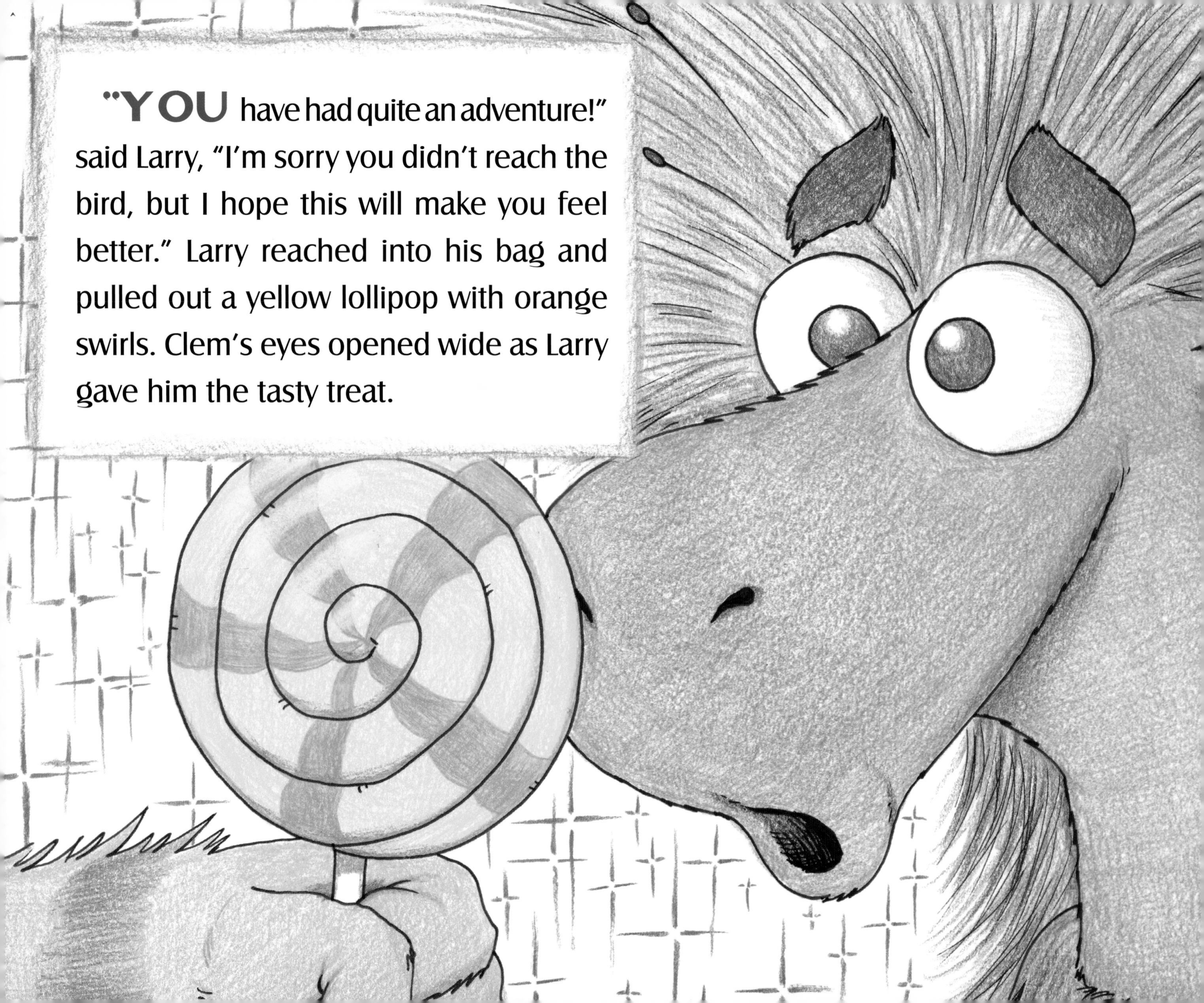

CLEM took the lollipop with both hands. "Wow!" he exclaimed, "What a wonderful gift!" He was so excited that he began to spin in circles while he stared at the beautiful lollipop. Round and round he went, spinning so fast that he lost his balance and fell into a nearby bush!

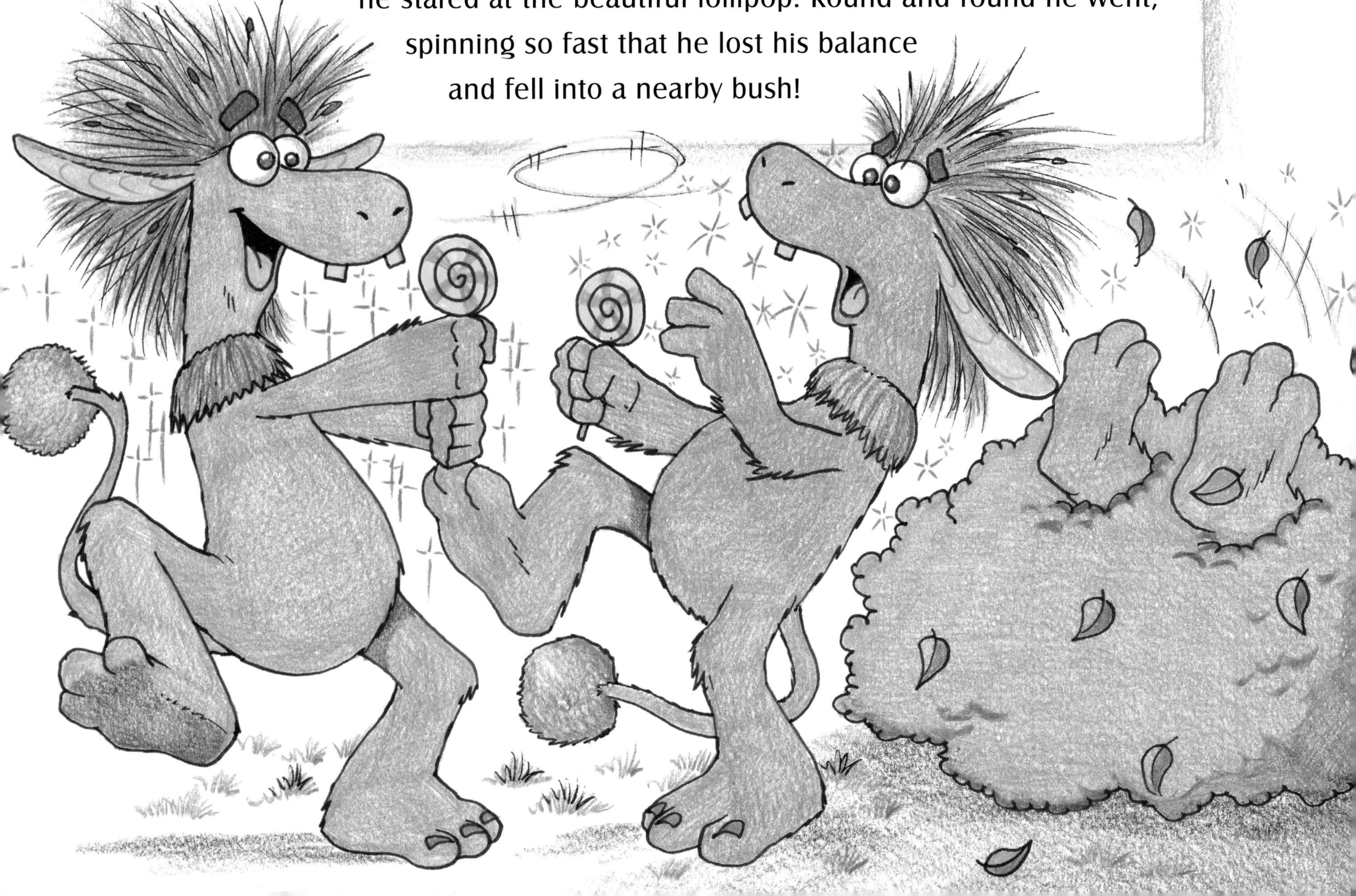

LARRY and Zabby rushed over and helped Clem up. "Are you okay, Clem?" Larry asked. Clem had an embarrassed look on his face. "I'm afraid I've done it again."

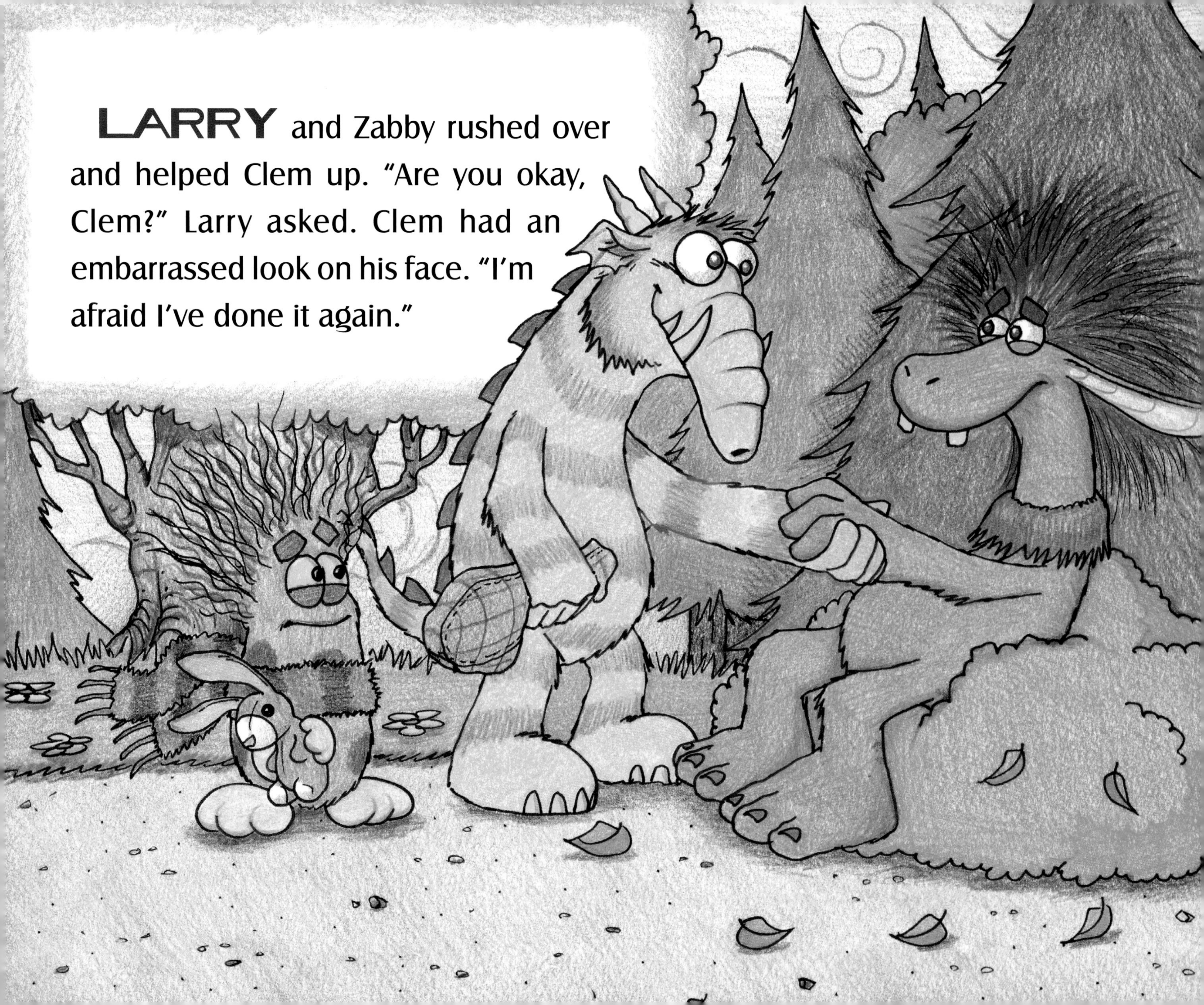

"I don't know why, but when I get excited, I can be such a klutz." He tried to put on a smile, then started to eat the lollipop.

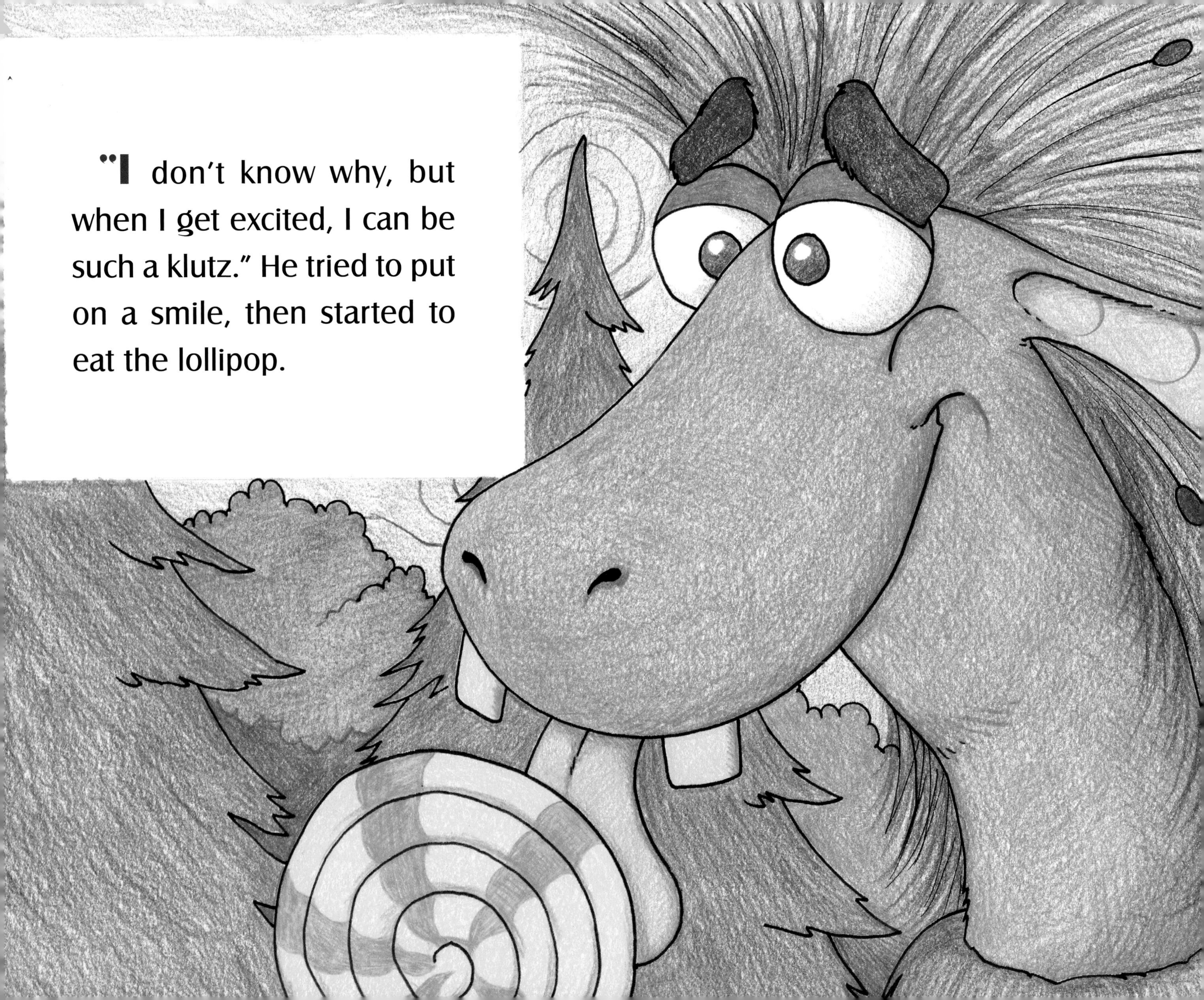

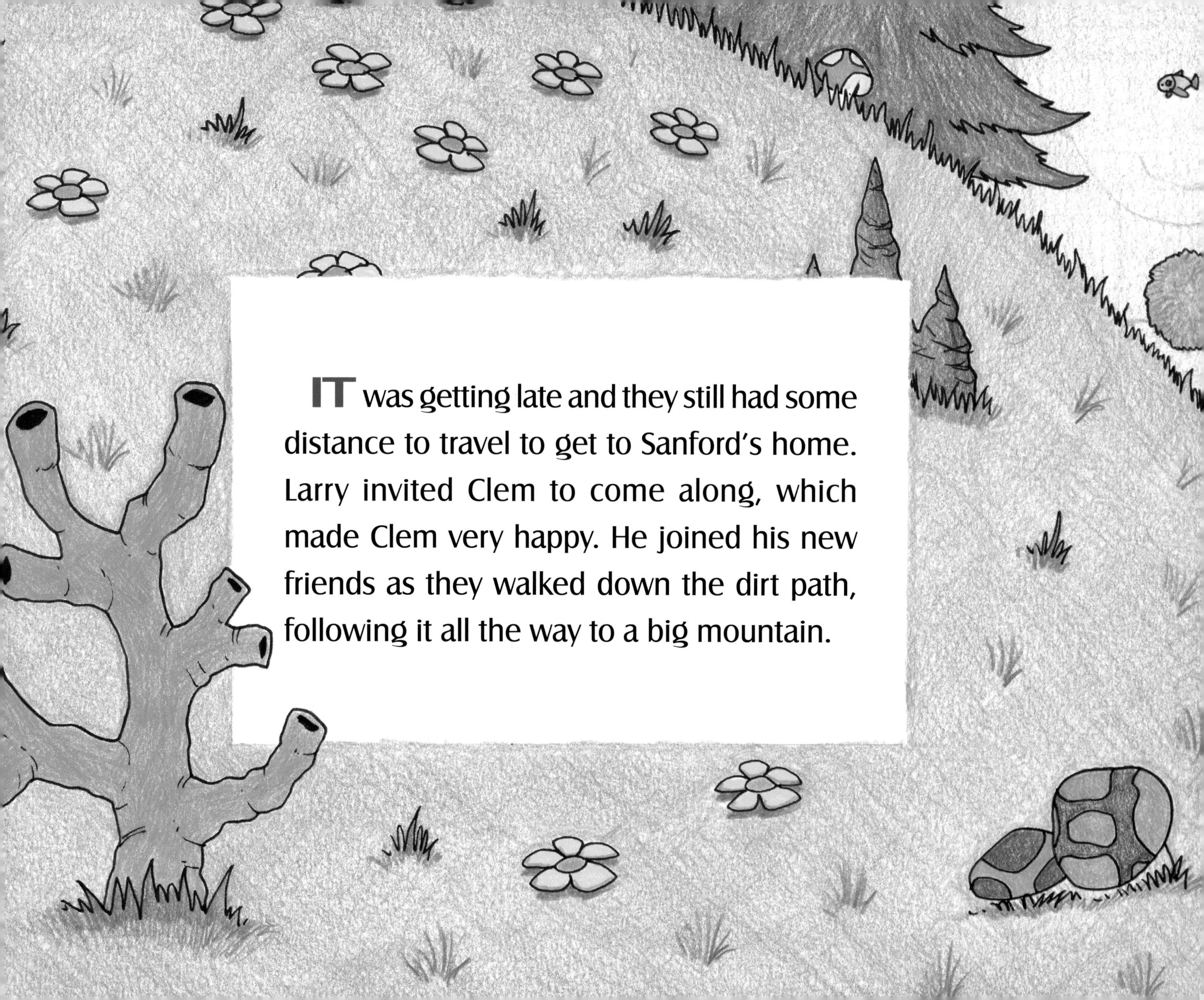

IT was getting late and they still had some distance to travel to get to Sanford's home. Larry invited Clem to come along, which made Clem very happy. He joined his new friends as they walked down the dirt path, following it all the way to a big mountain.

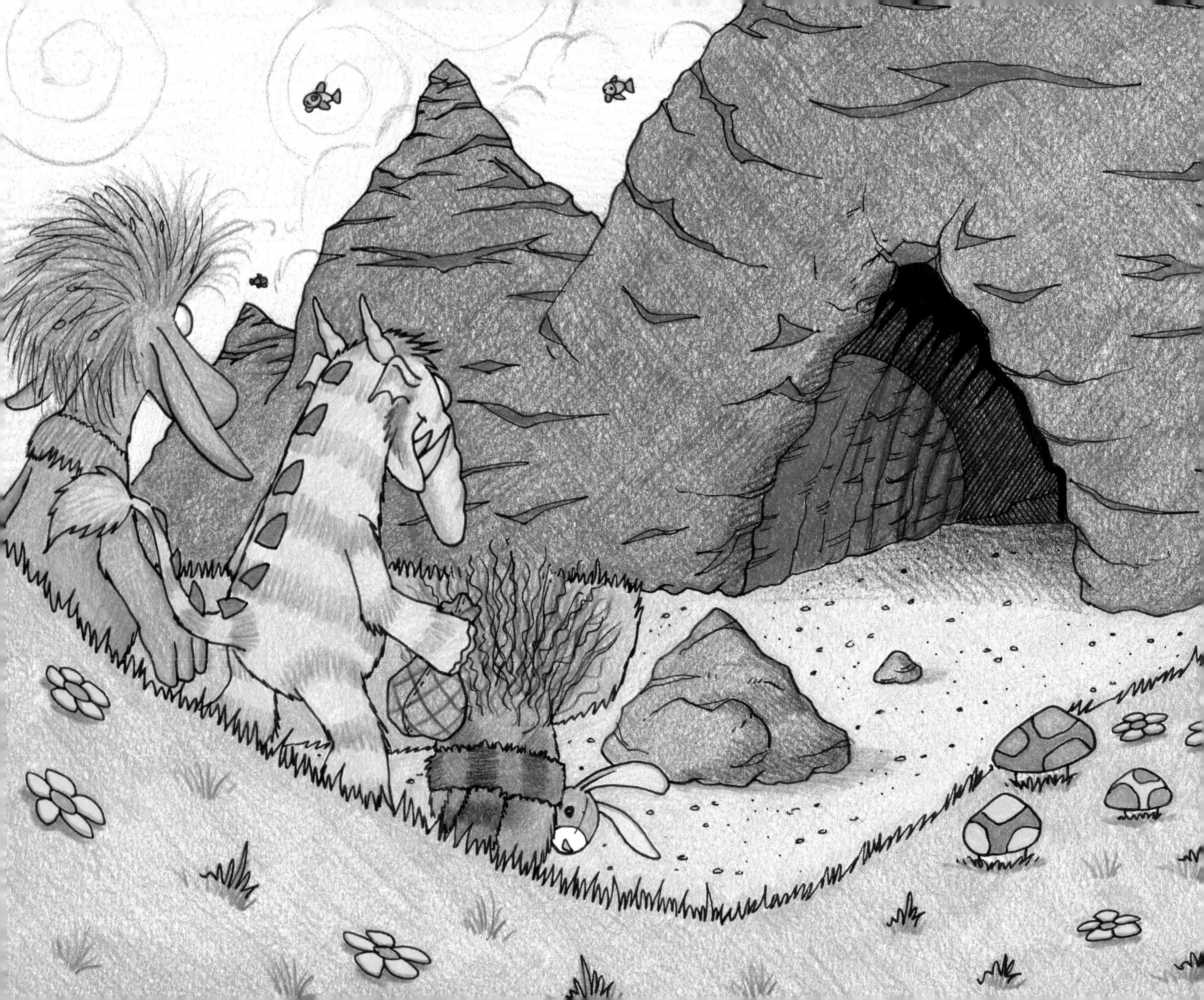

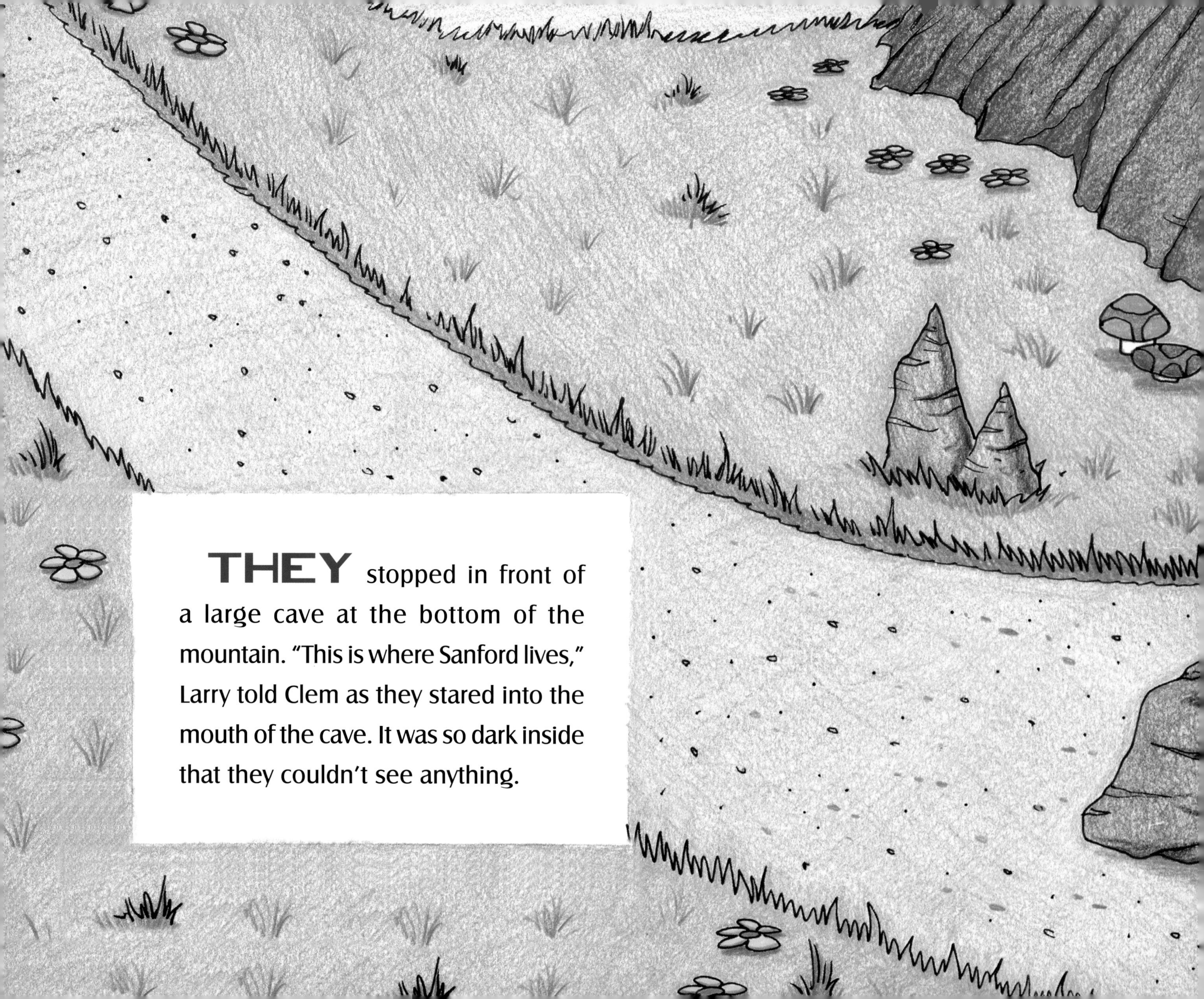

THEY stopped in front of a large cave at the bottom of the mountain. “This is where Sanford lives,” Larry told Clem as they stared into the mouth of the cave. It was so dark inside that they couldn’t see anything.

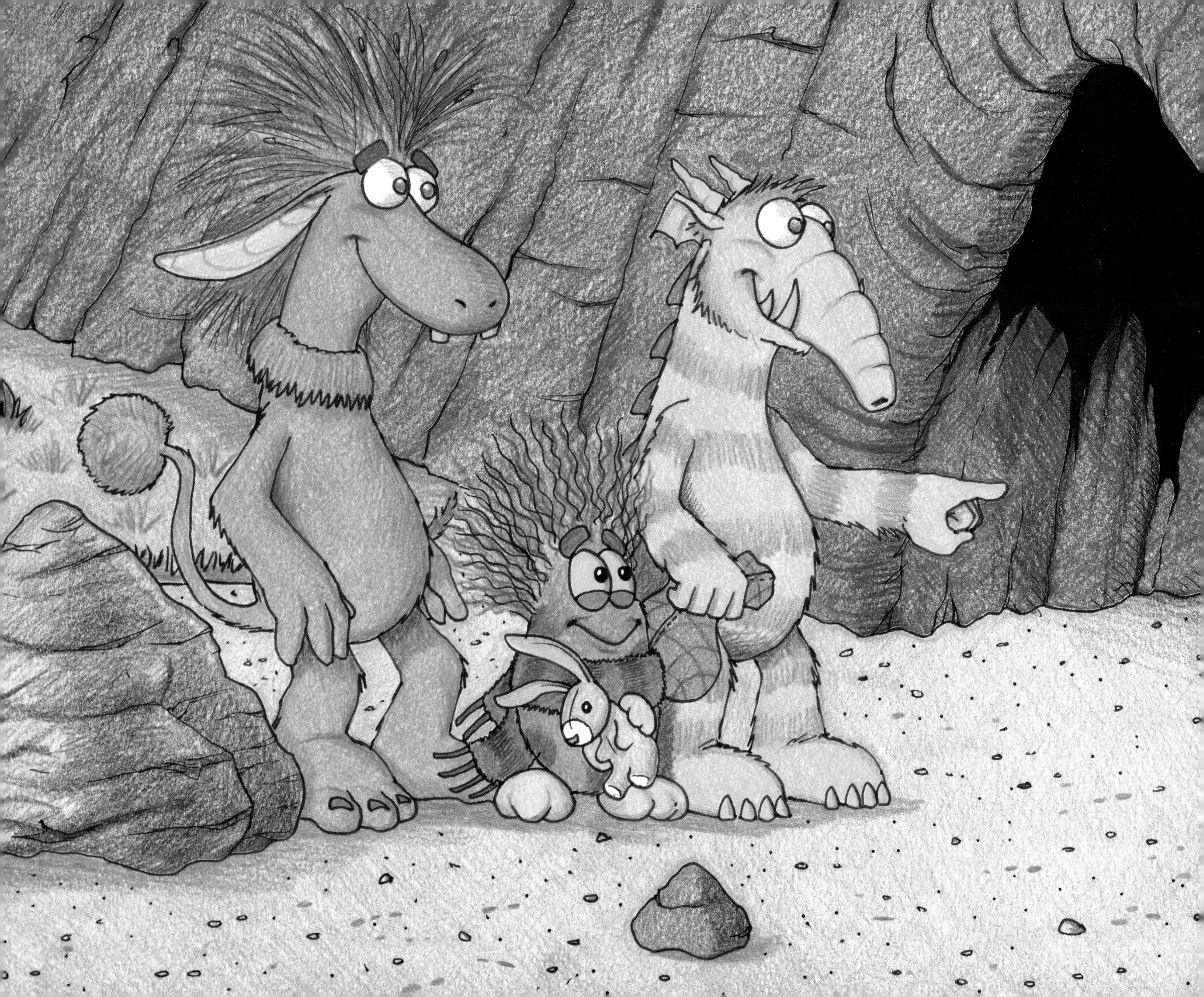

"**THIS** is going to be such a great surprise!" Larry exclaimed. "I can't wait to see the look on Sanford's face!"

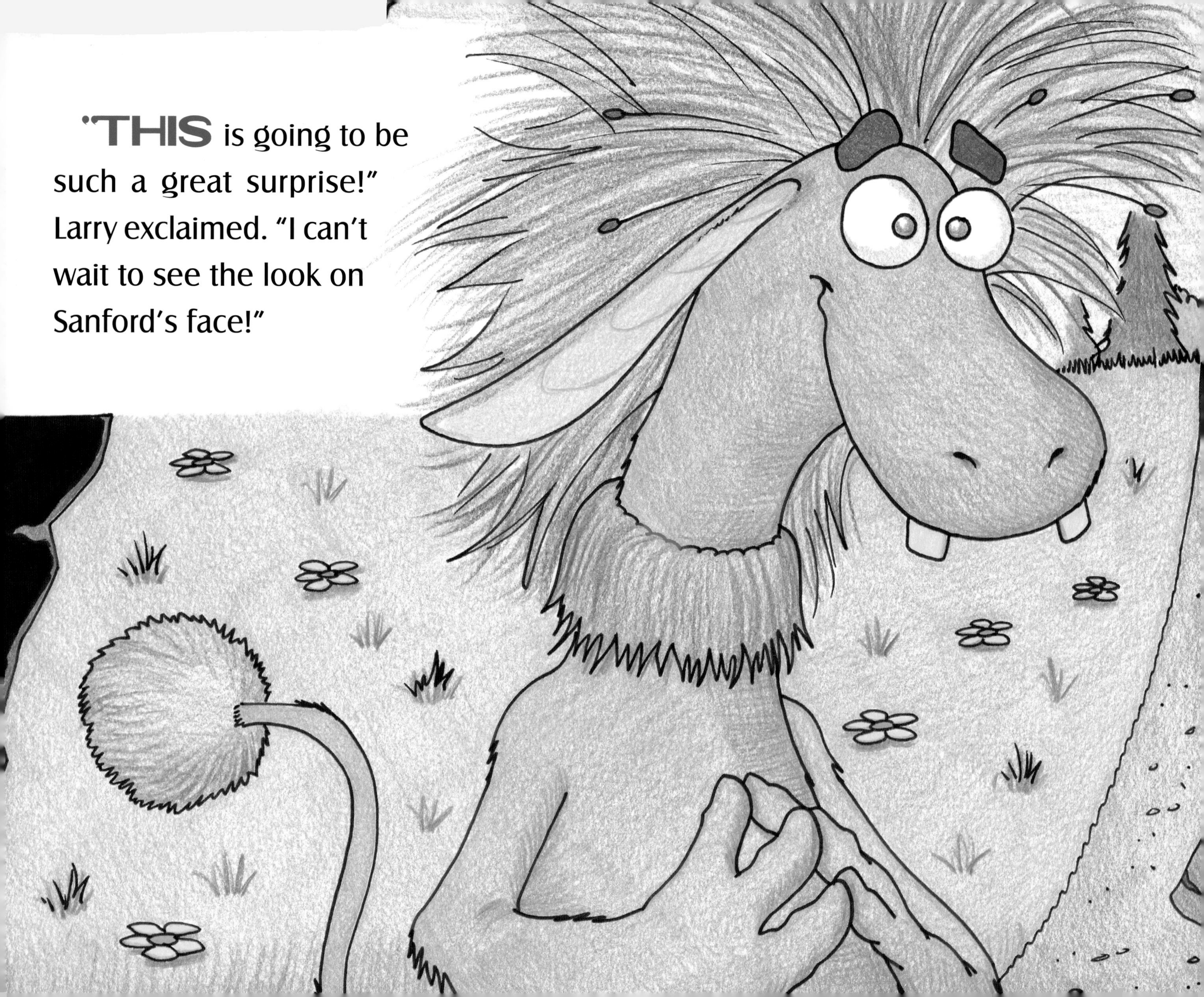

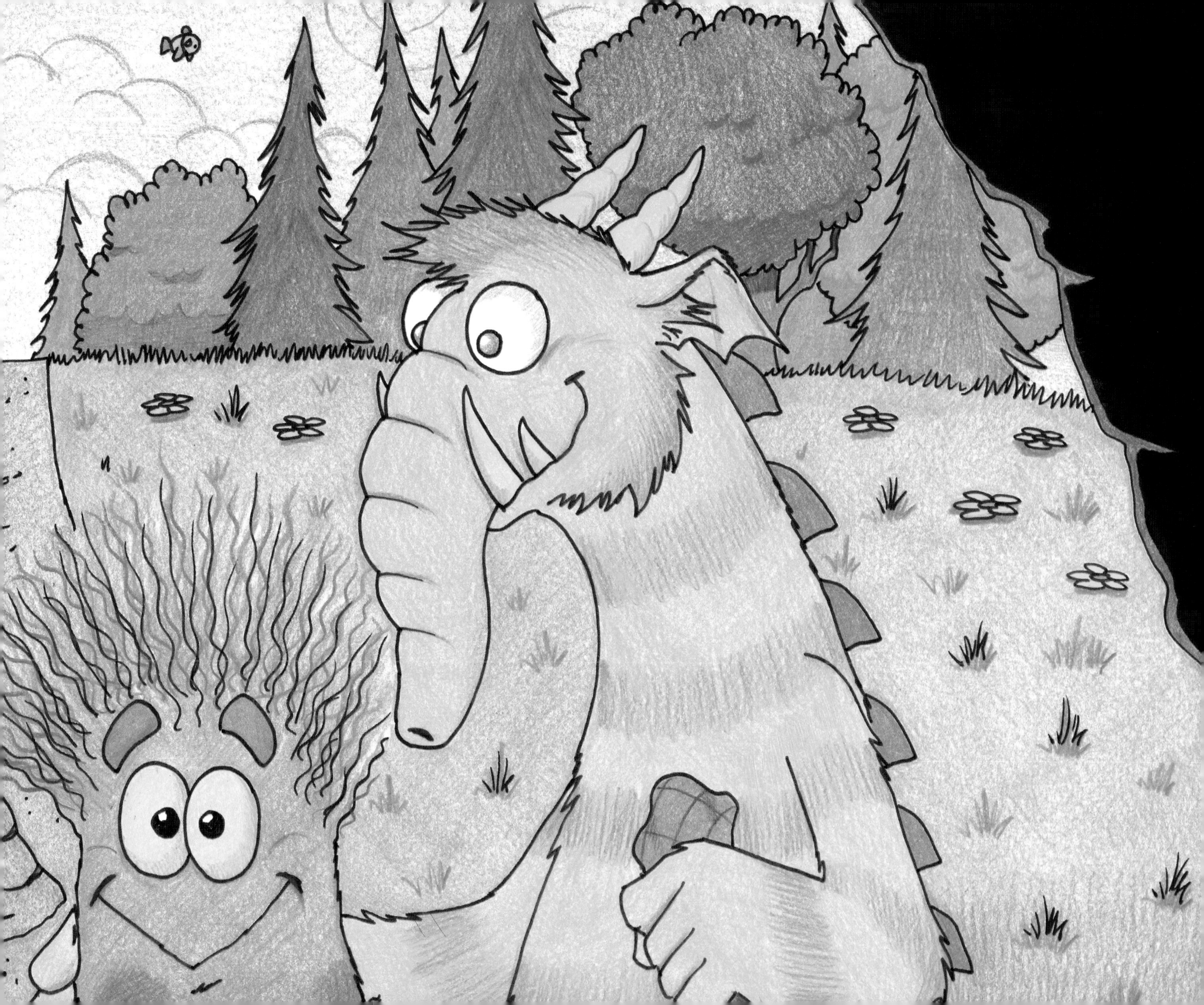

LARRY cupped his hands to his mouth and shouted…"Happy birthday, Sanford! Happy birthday to you!"

IN a flash, an orange, scaly monster appeared at the mouth of the cave. Sanford had a little red beard and eyes that seemed to float above his head on thin, orange stems. His big, toothy grin made it clear that he was happy to see Larry and Zabby.

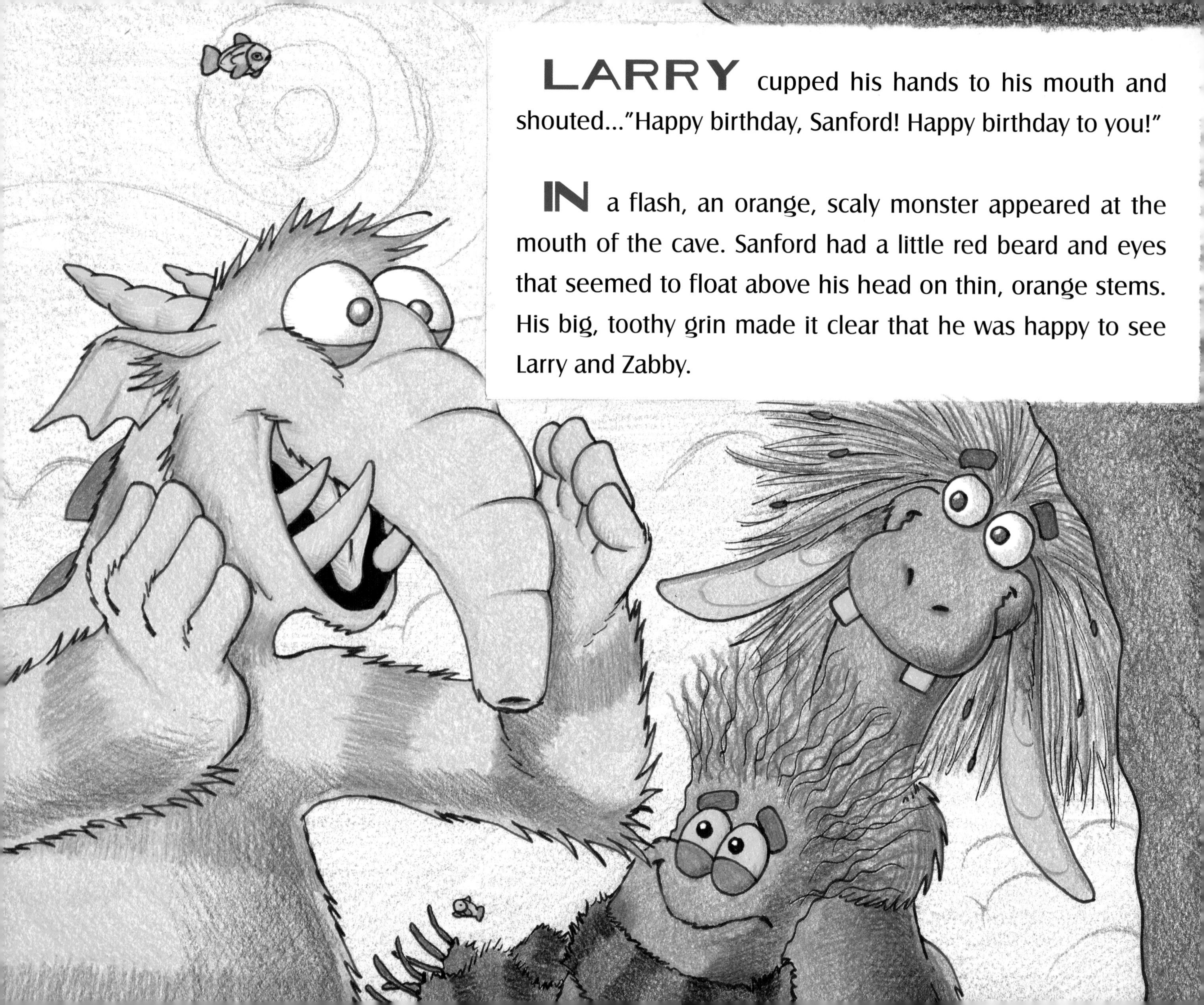

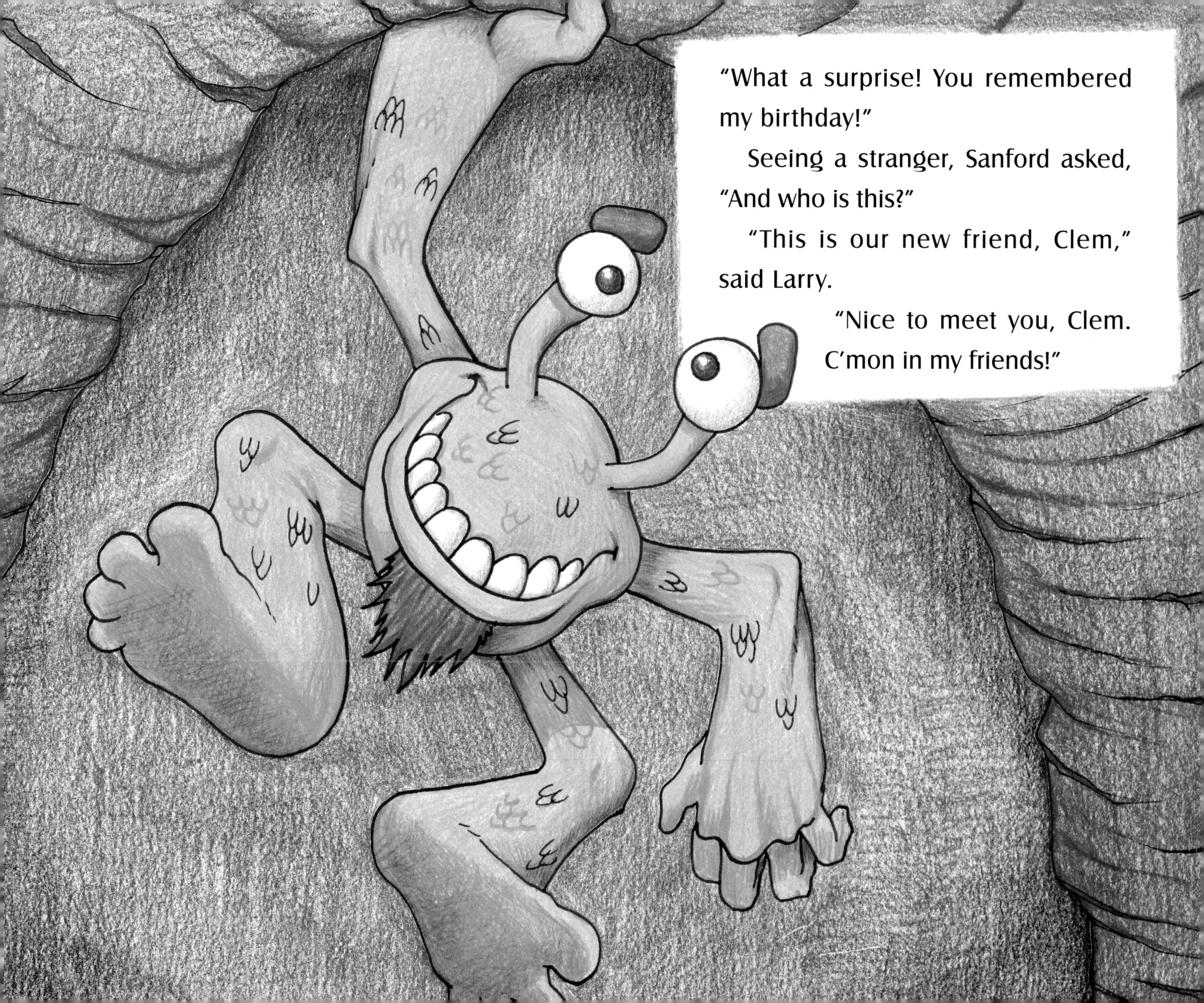

"What a surprise! You remembered my birthday!"

Seeing a stranger, Sanford asked, "And who is this?"

"This is our new friend, Clem," said Larry.

"Nice to meet you, Clem. C'mon in my friends!"

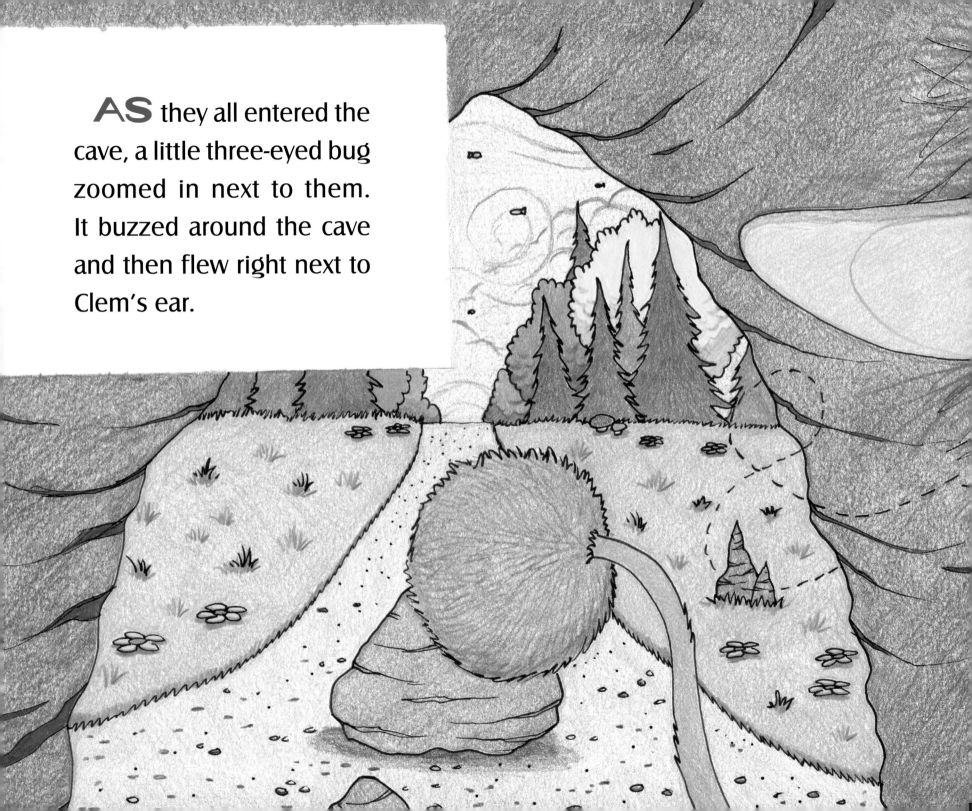

AS they all entered the cave, a little three-eyed bug zoomed in next to them. It buzzed around the cave and then flew right next to Clem's ear.

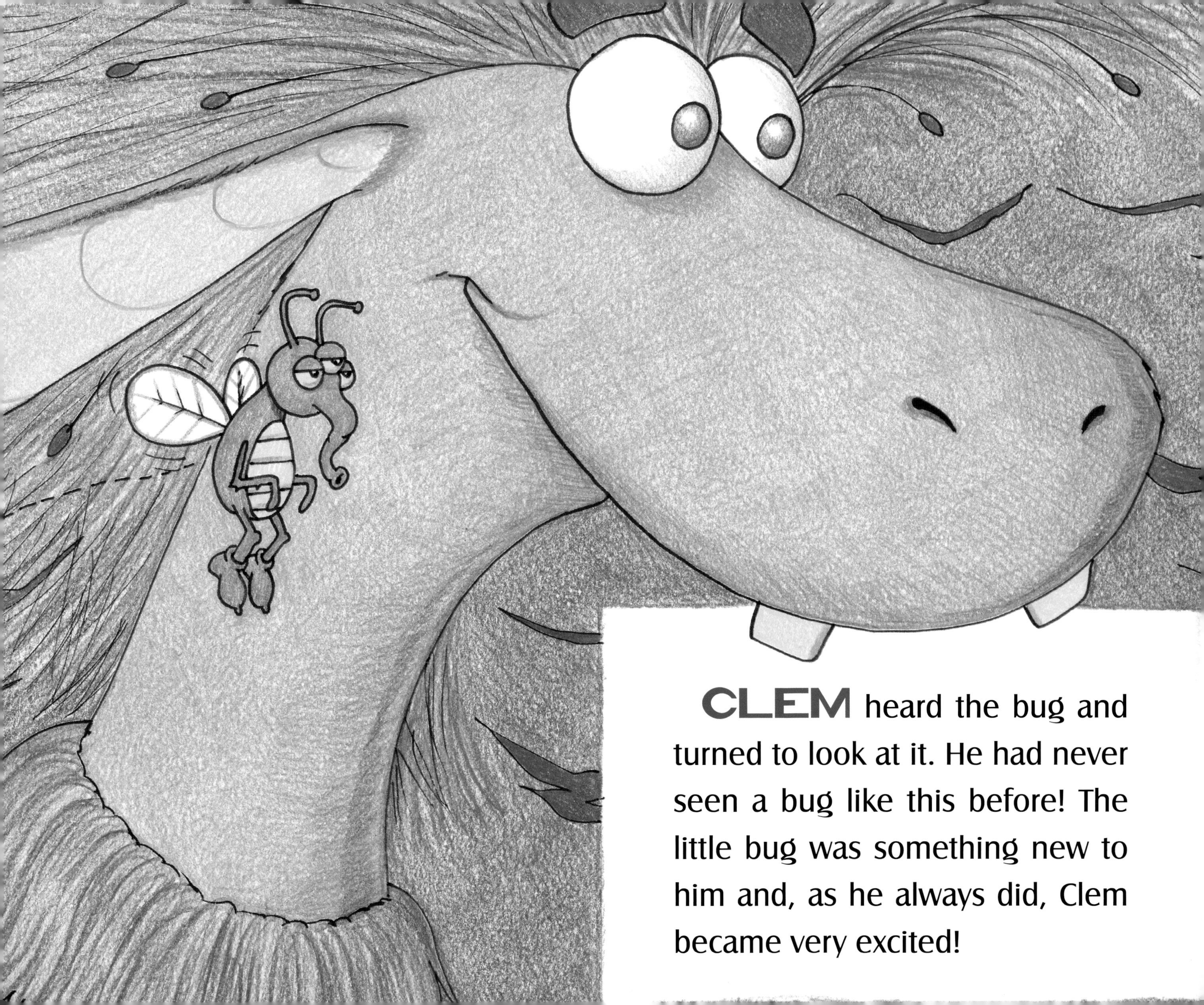

CLEM heard the bug and turned to look at it. He had never seen a bug like this before! The little bug was something new to him and, as he always did, Clem became very excited!

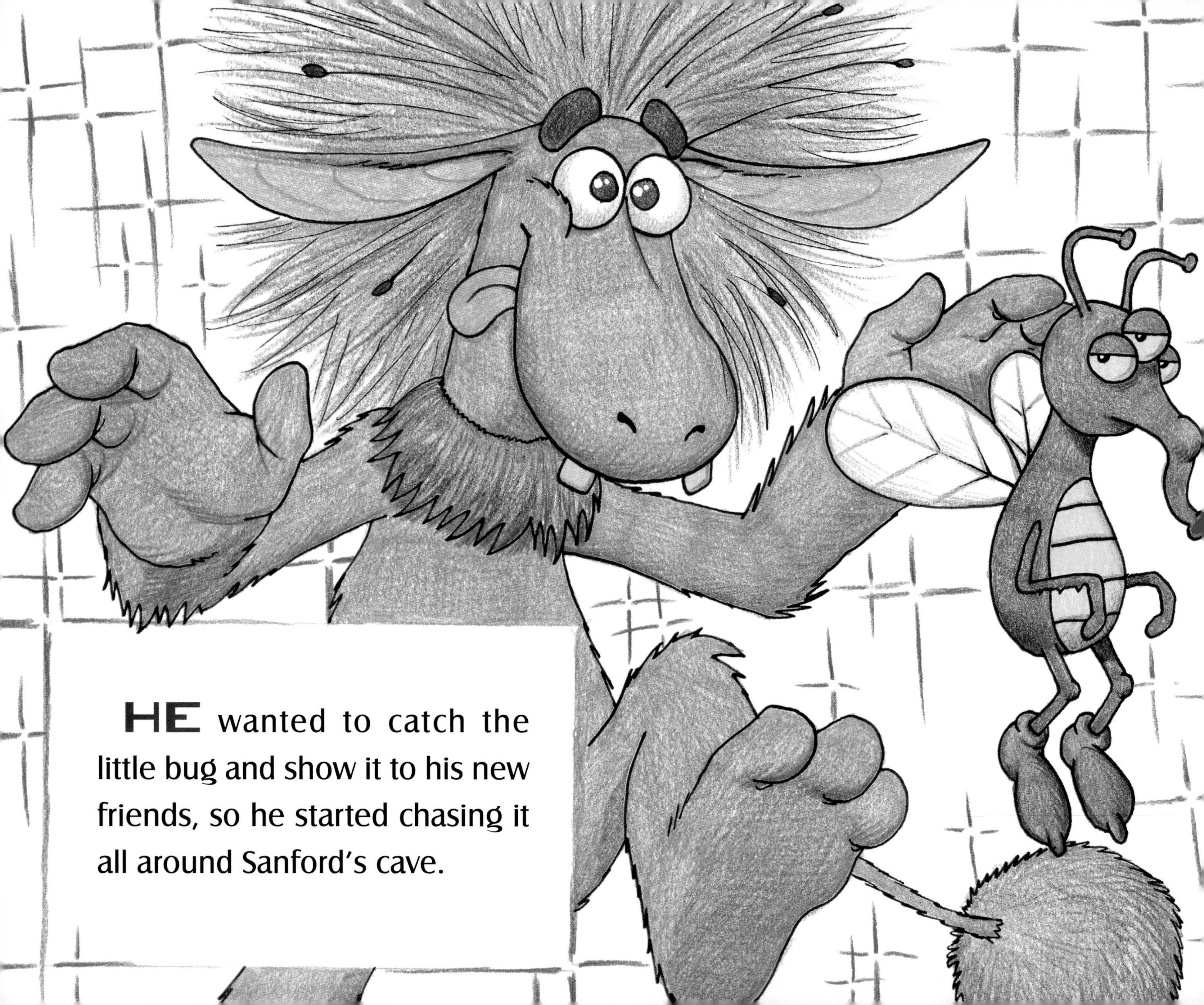

HE wanted to catch the little bug and show it to his new friends, so he started chasing it all around Sanford's cave.

THE little bug flew up and down, left and right, with Clem following him so closely that he didn't look where he was going. He had almost reached the bug when he tripped over a small wooden stool and fell on his head.

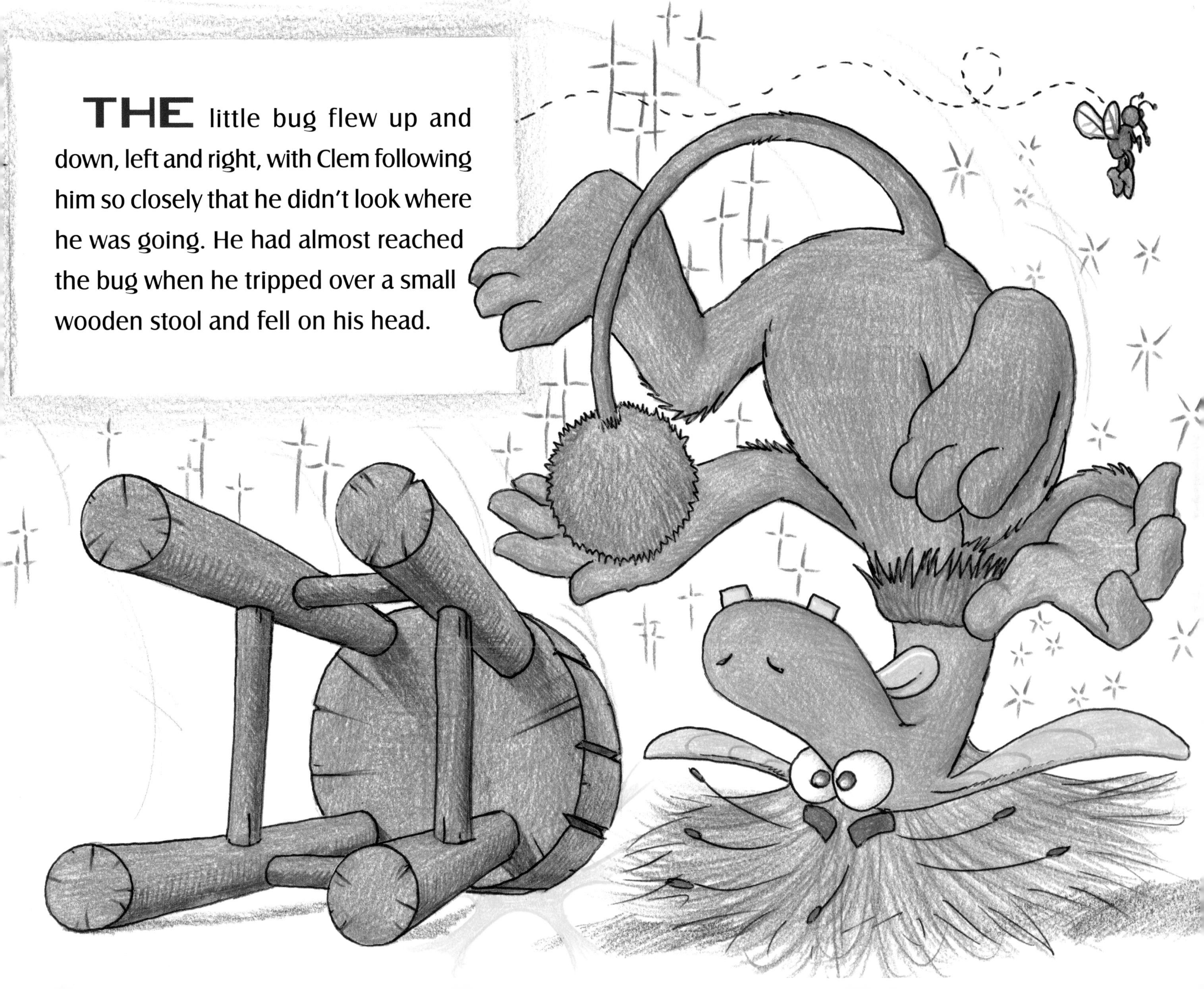

SANFORD ran over to Clem and helped him up. "Are you okay?" he asked. Once again, Clem was embarrassed for being silly and falling down. "I am so sorry…I can be so clumsy."

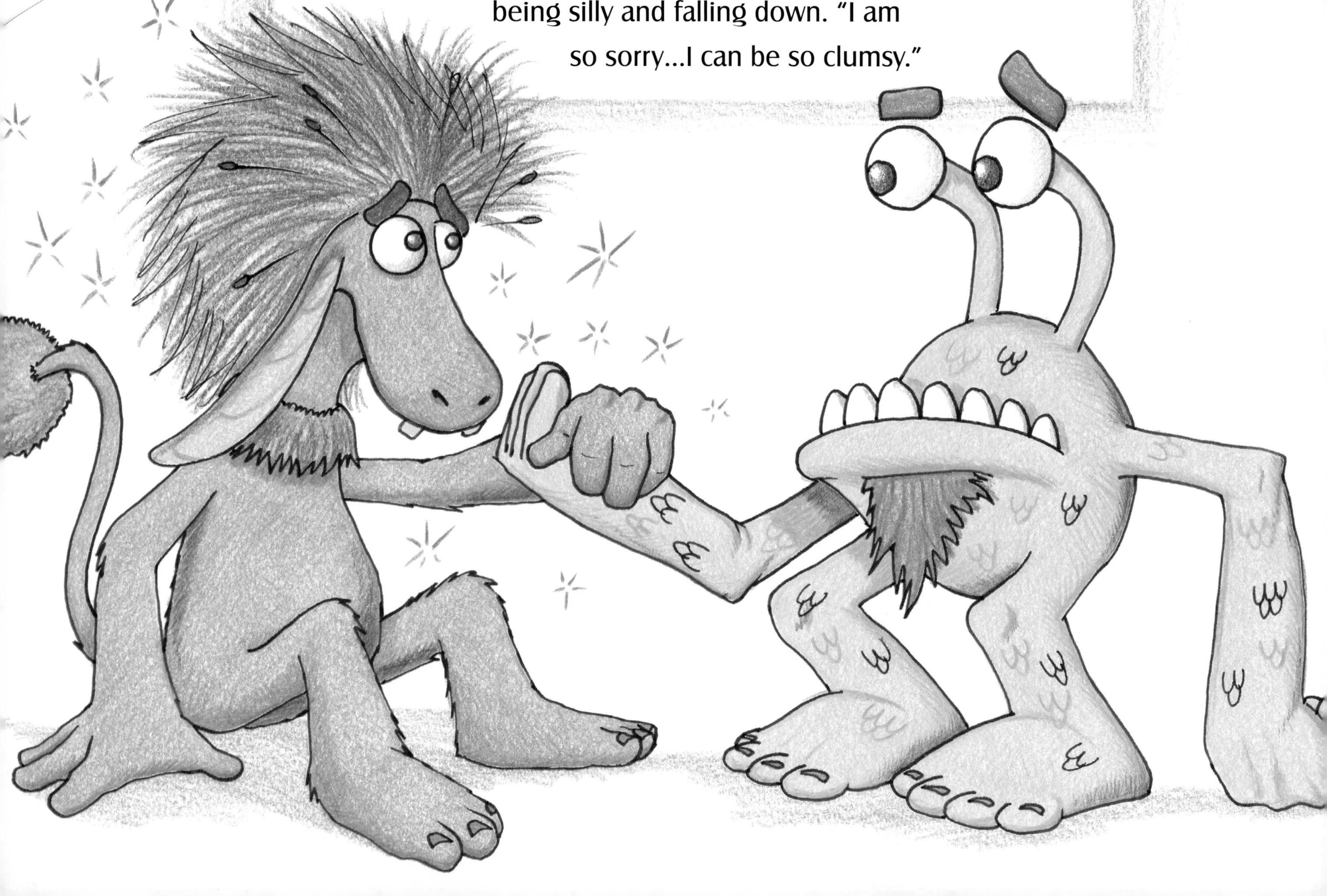

CLEM was not hurt, and neither was the bug, so, before anything else could happen, Larry reached into his brown lollipop sack and presented Sanford with his birthday present. "Zabby and I have a surprise for you!"

Sanford looked at the giant blue lollipop and was very happy. "Wow! That's just what I wanted! Thank you so much, Larry and Zabby!"

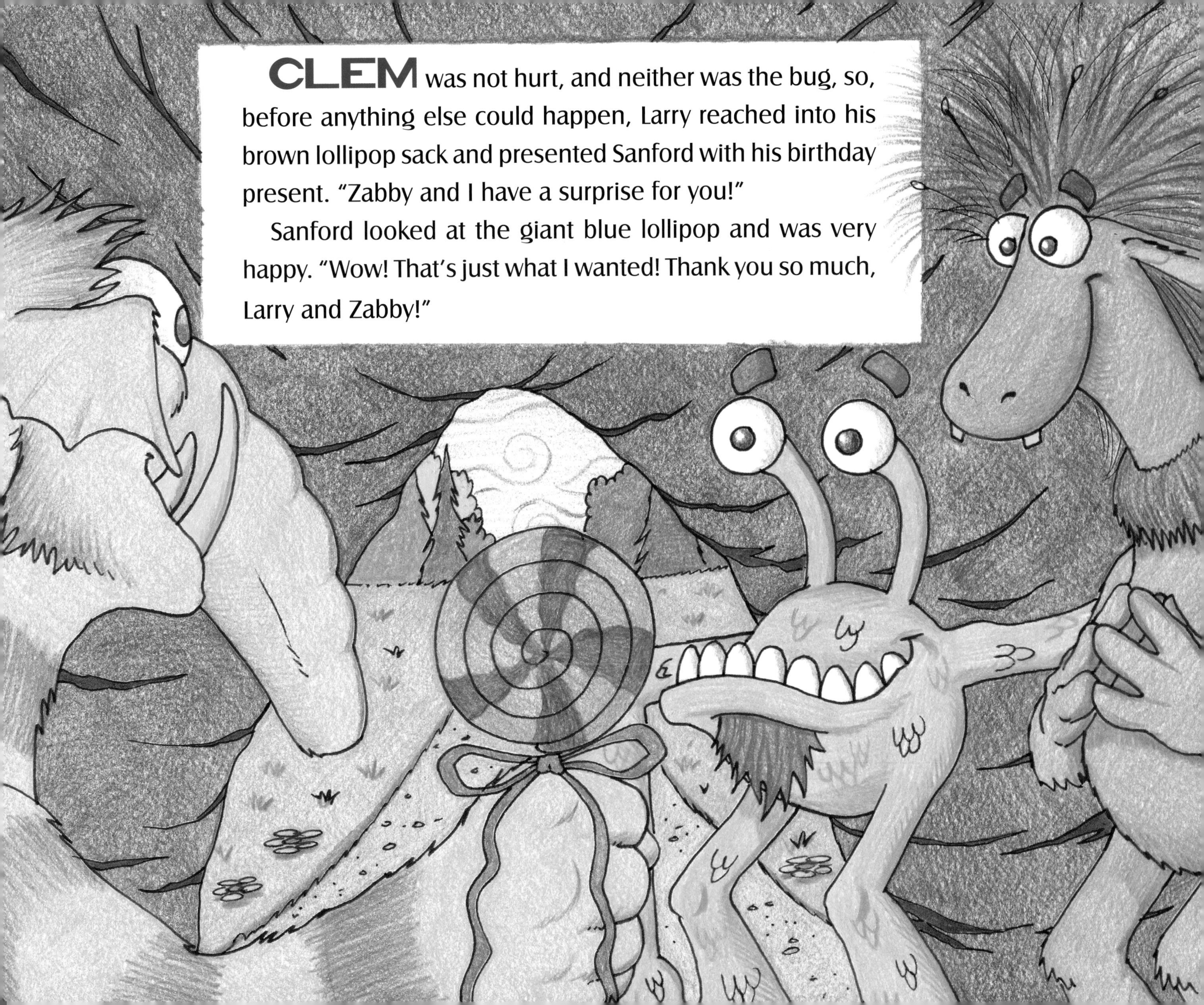

CLEM was looking at the lollipop, too, and as Larry started to hand the lollipop over to Sanford, Clem began to get excited. A large smile spread across his face.

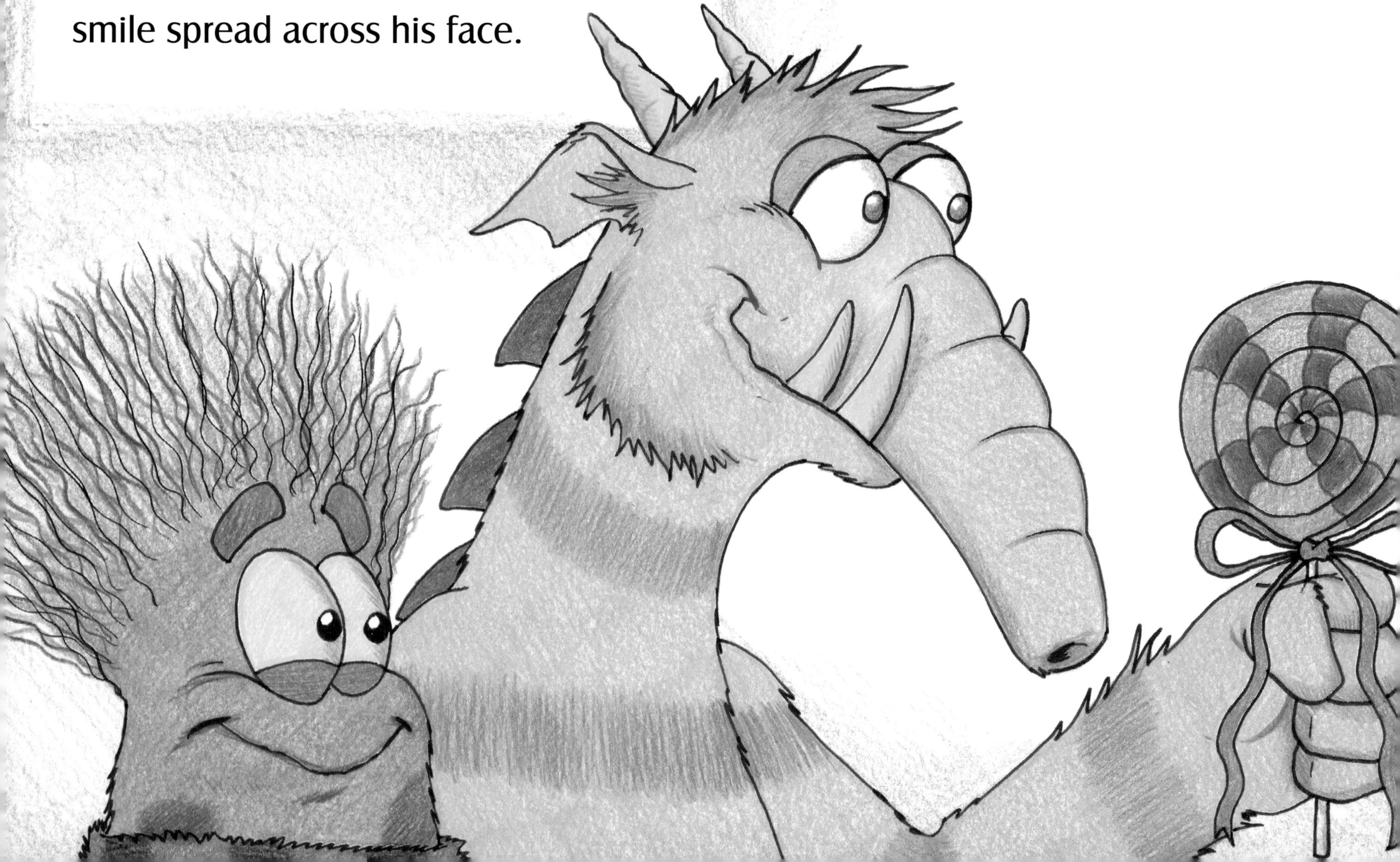

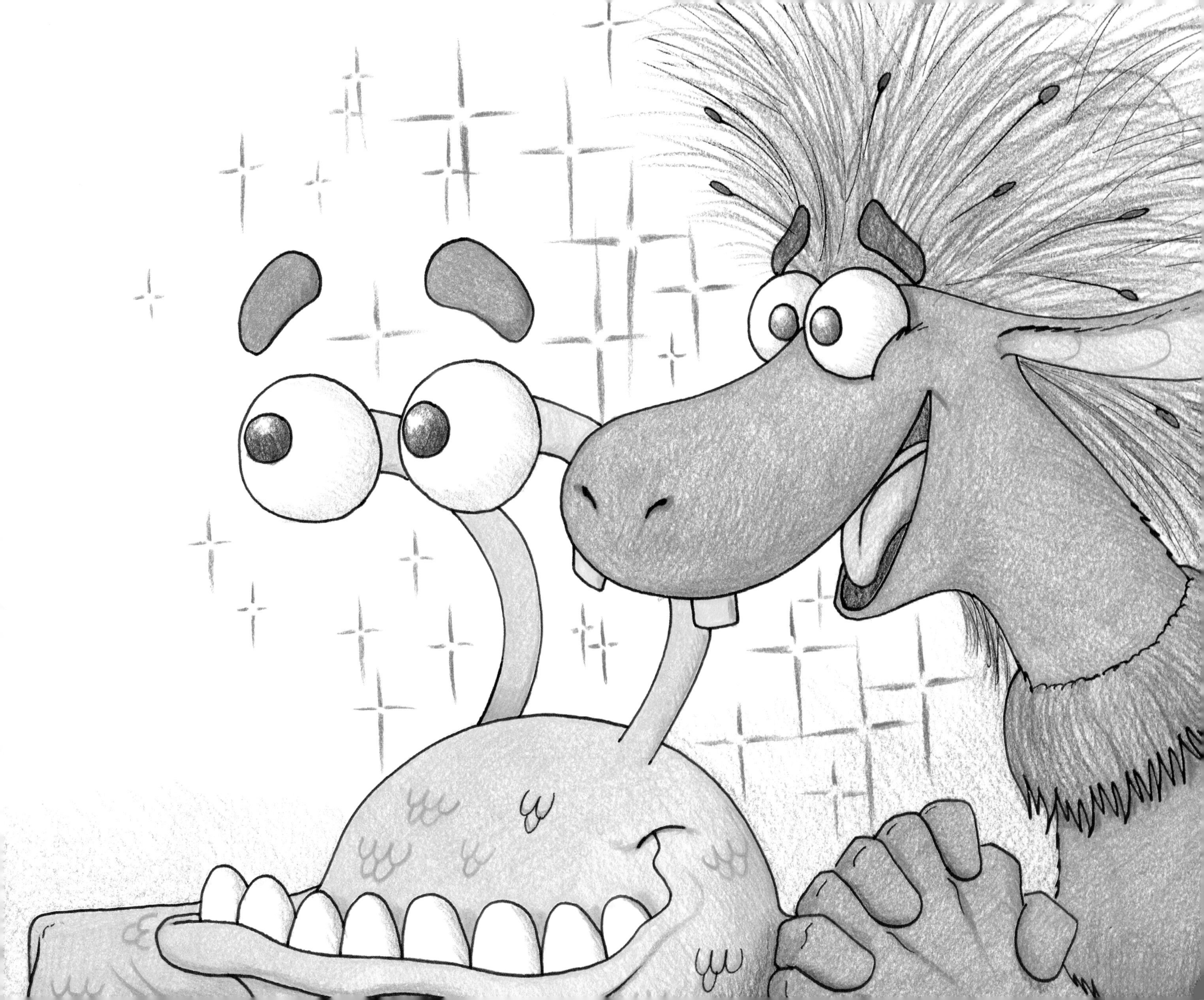

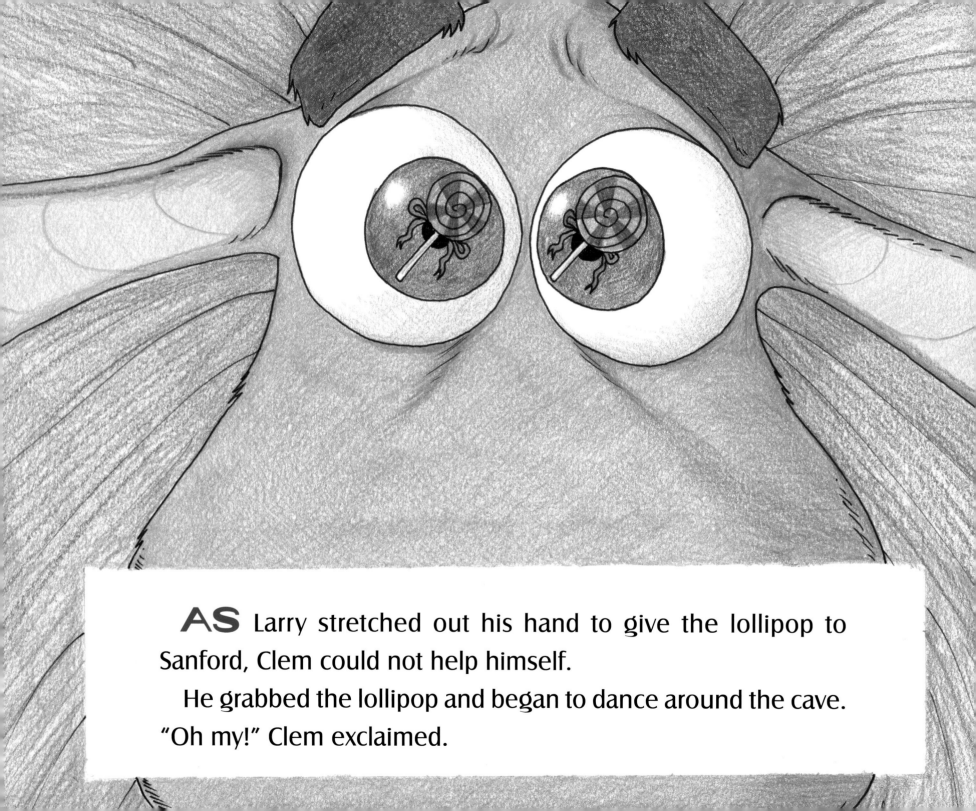

AS Larry stretched out his hand to give the lollipop to Sanford, Clem could not help himself.

He grabbed the lollipop and began to dance around the cave. "Oh my!" Clem exclaimed.

"**HAVE** you ever seen such a beautiful lollipop before? Gosh, Larry...you and Zabby did such a wonderful job. I'm sure Sanford is going to love this!"

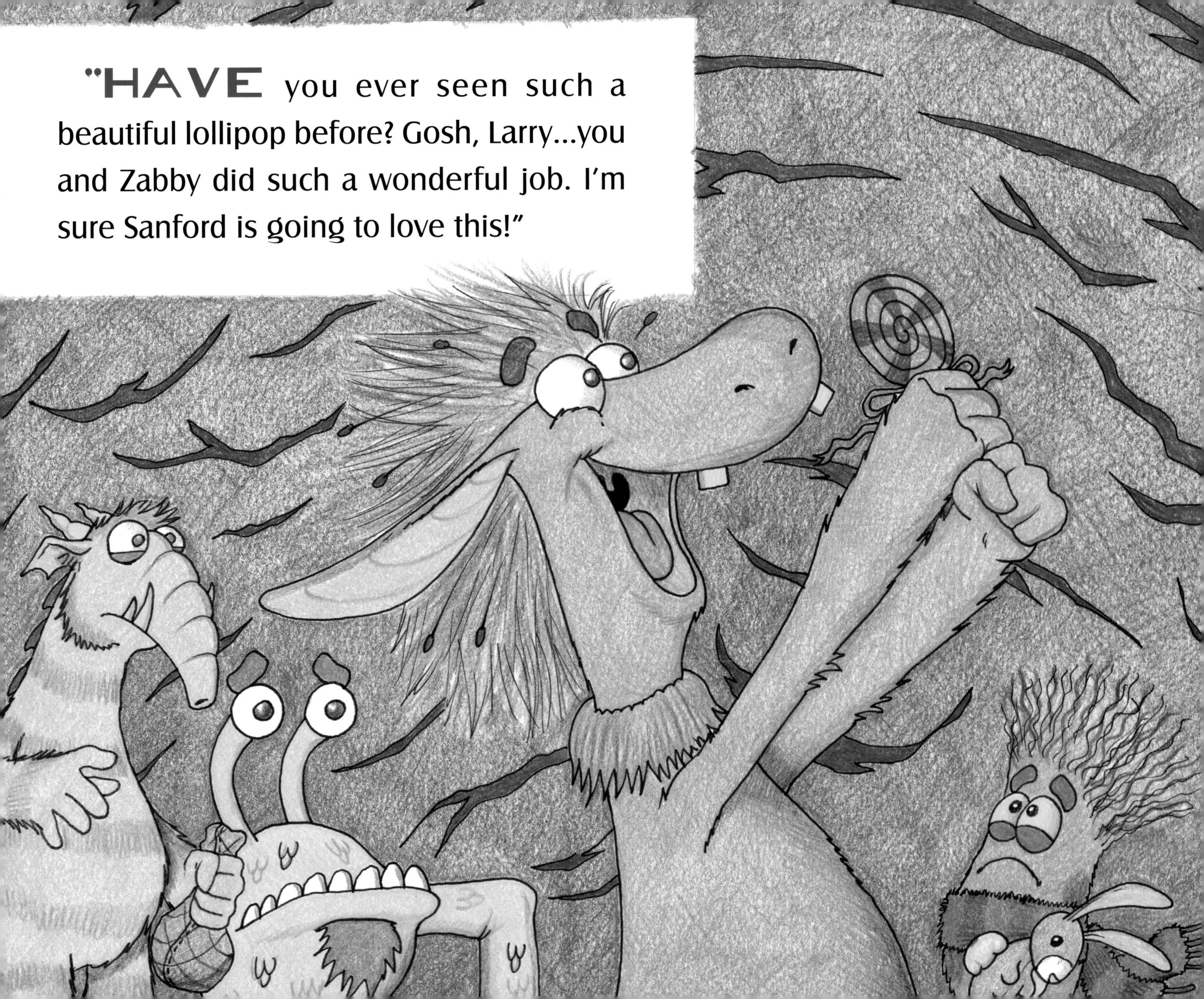

AS Clem became more and more excited, he started to spin, twirling in a circle and admiring the beautiful treat. Clem's friends watched in horror as his long tail got tangled around his leg and he started to lose his balance.

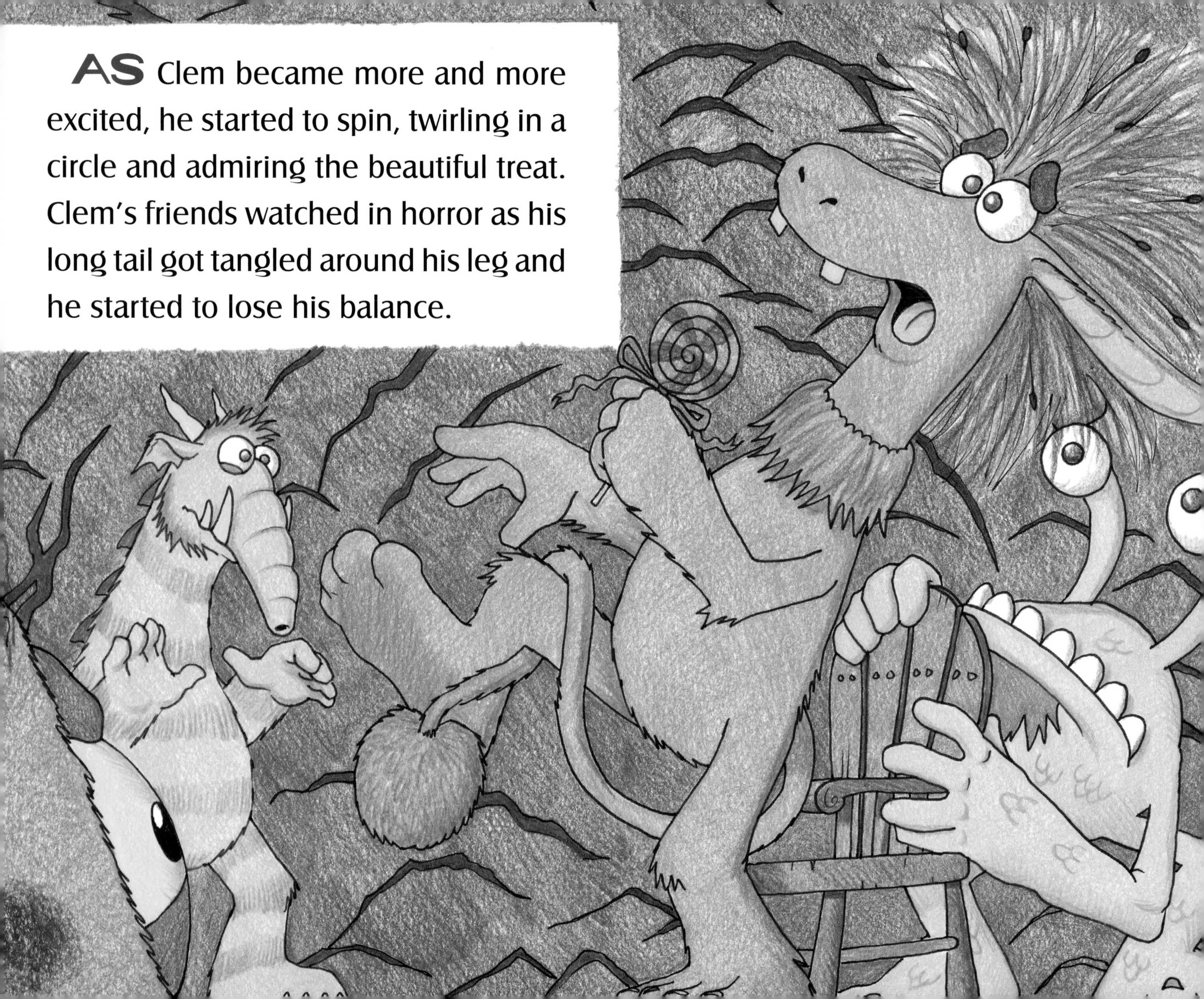

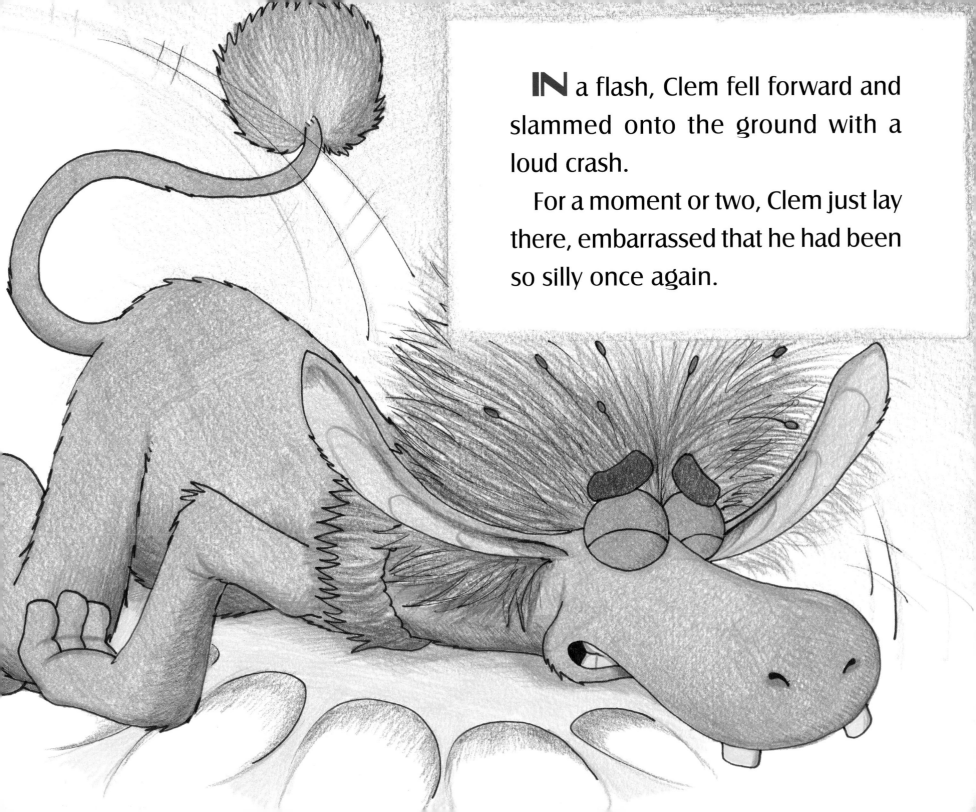

IN a flash, Clem fell forward and slammed onto the ground with a loud crash.

For a moment or two, Clem just lay there, embarrassed that he had been so silly once again.

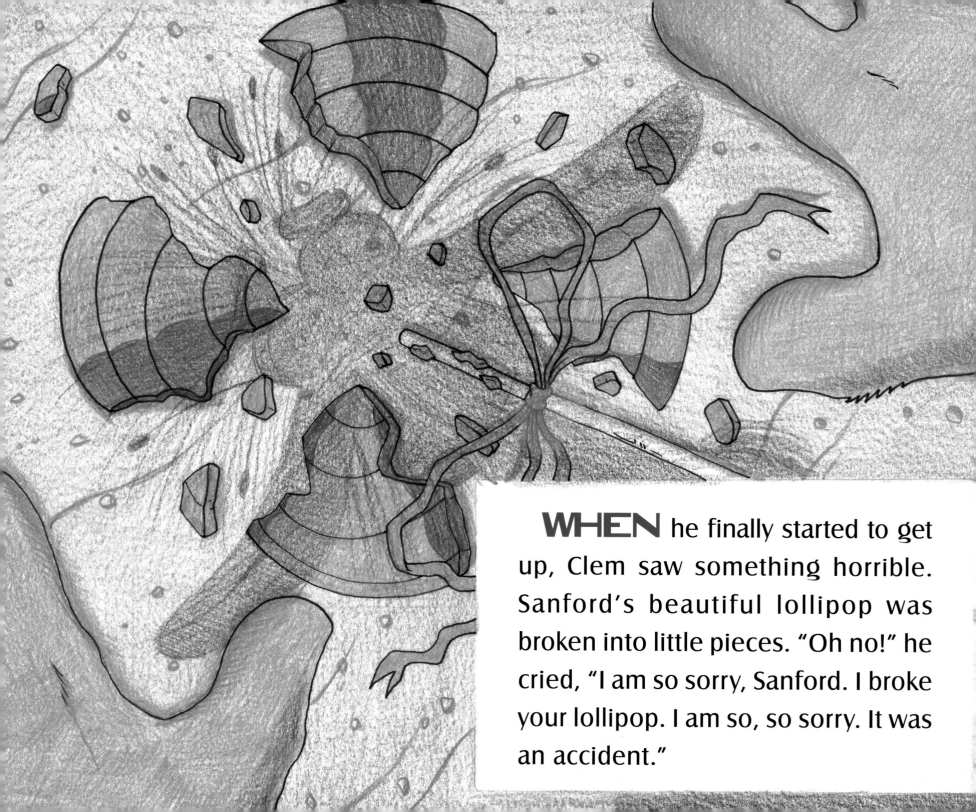

WHEN he finally started to get up, Clem saw something horrible. Sanford's beautiful lollipop was broken into little pieces. "Oh no!" he cried, "I am so sorry, Sanford. I broke your lollipop. I am so, so sorry. It was an accident."

SANFORD really loved his birthday present and found himself becoming very angry with the clumsy monster. "You big dummy! Look what you did to my present!," he shouted, "You broke it! You really are a klutz, Clem!"

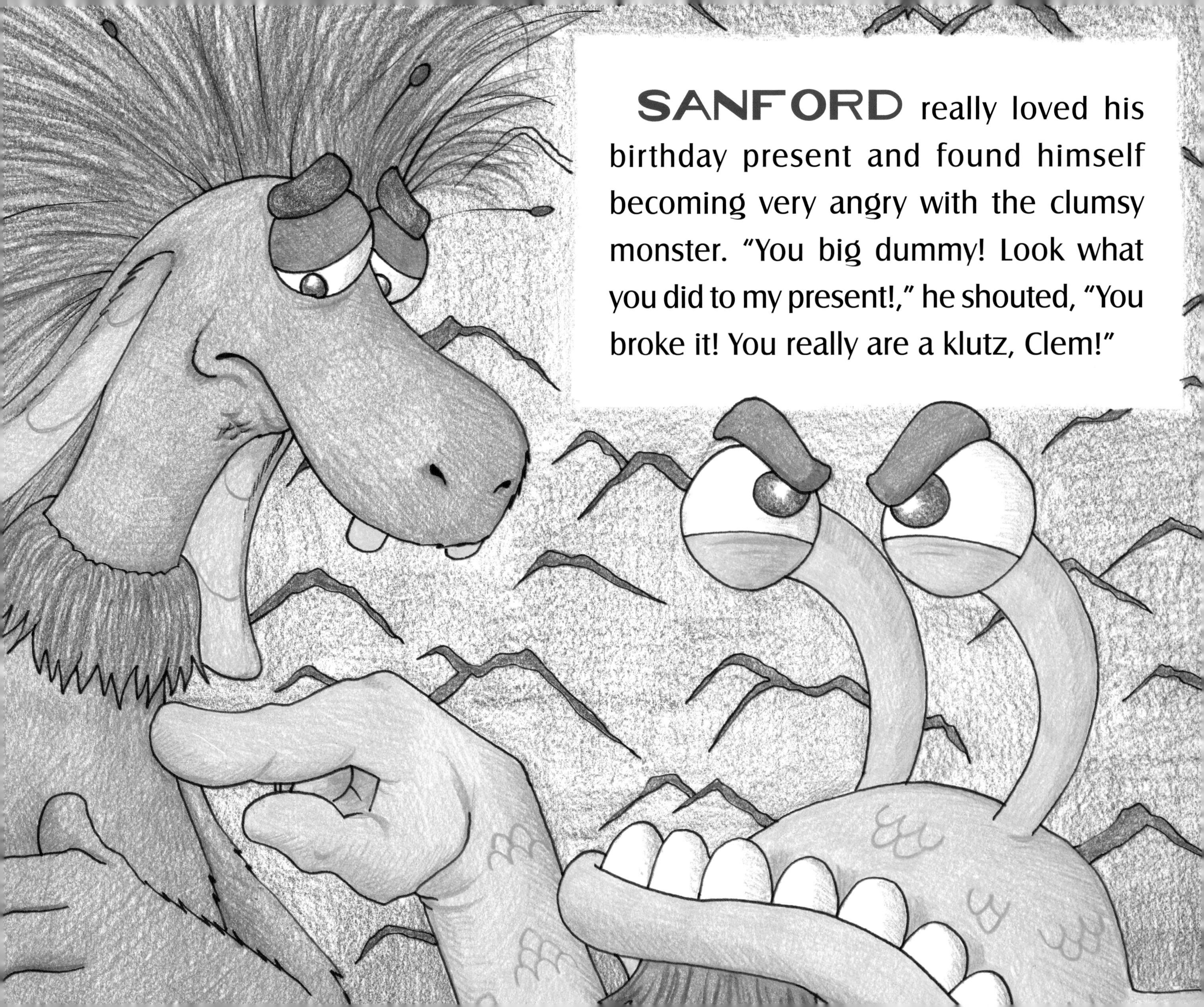

CLEM had never felt so bad. "You're right, Sanford. I am a dummy and a klutz. Everywhere I go I always do something to ruin a good thing. I'm sorry I spoiled your birthday." Clem lowered his head and went outside. He just wanted to be alone.

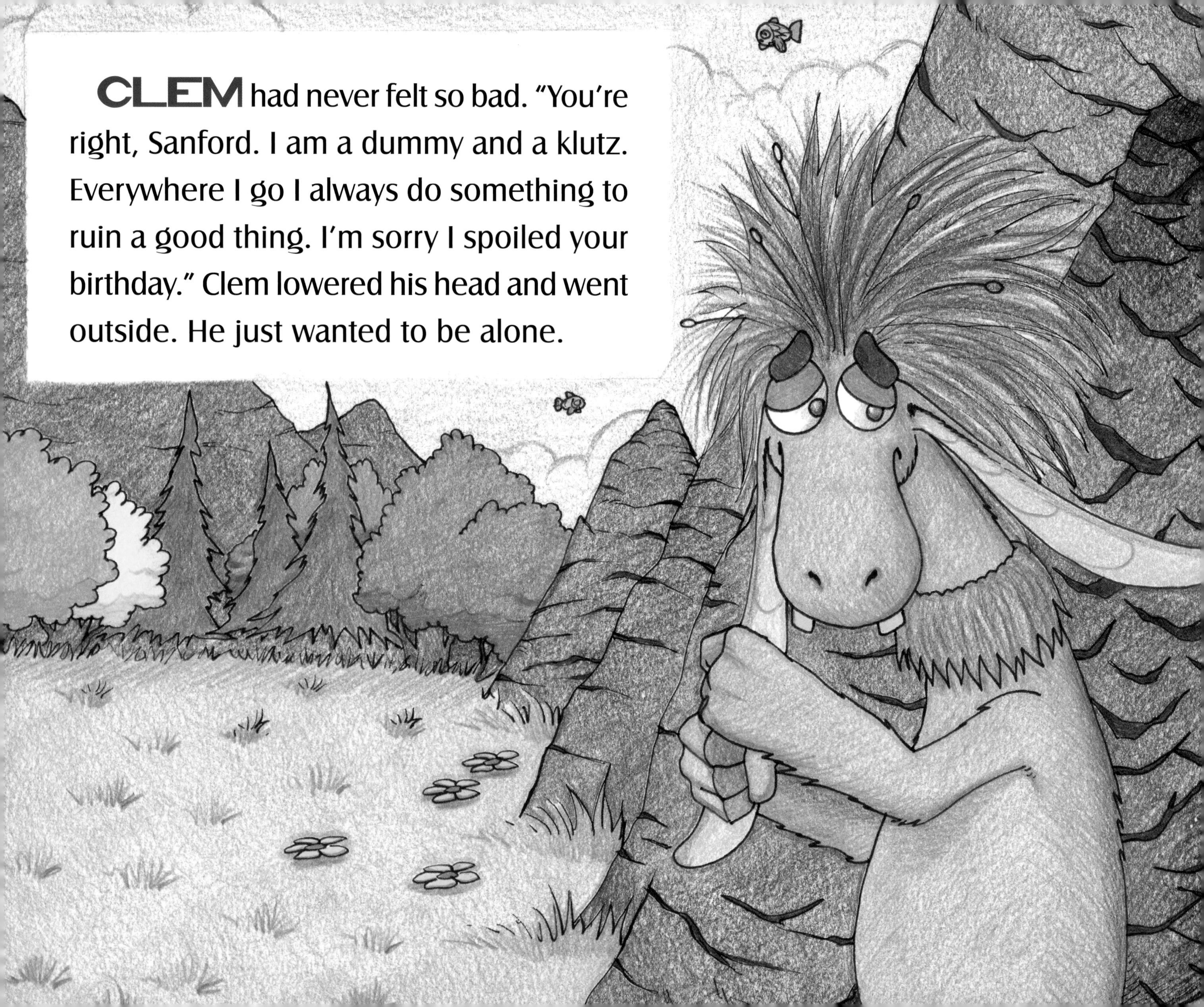

BACK in the cave, Larry put his arm around Sanford. "I know you are angry, Sanford, but I don't think calling him names was the right thing to do. I'm sure it was an accident. It's okay to be upset, but maybe you should think about how much it can hurt someone when you call them names."

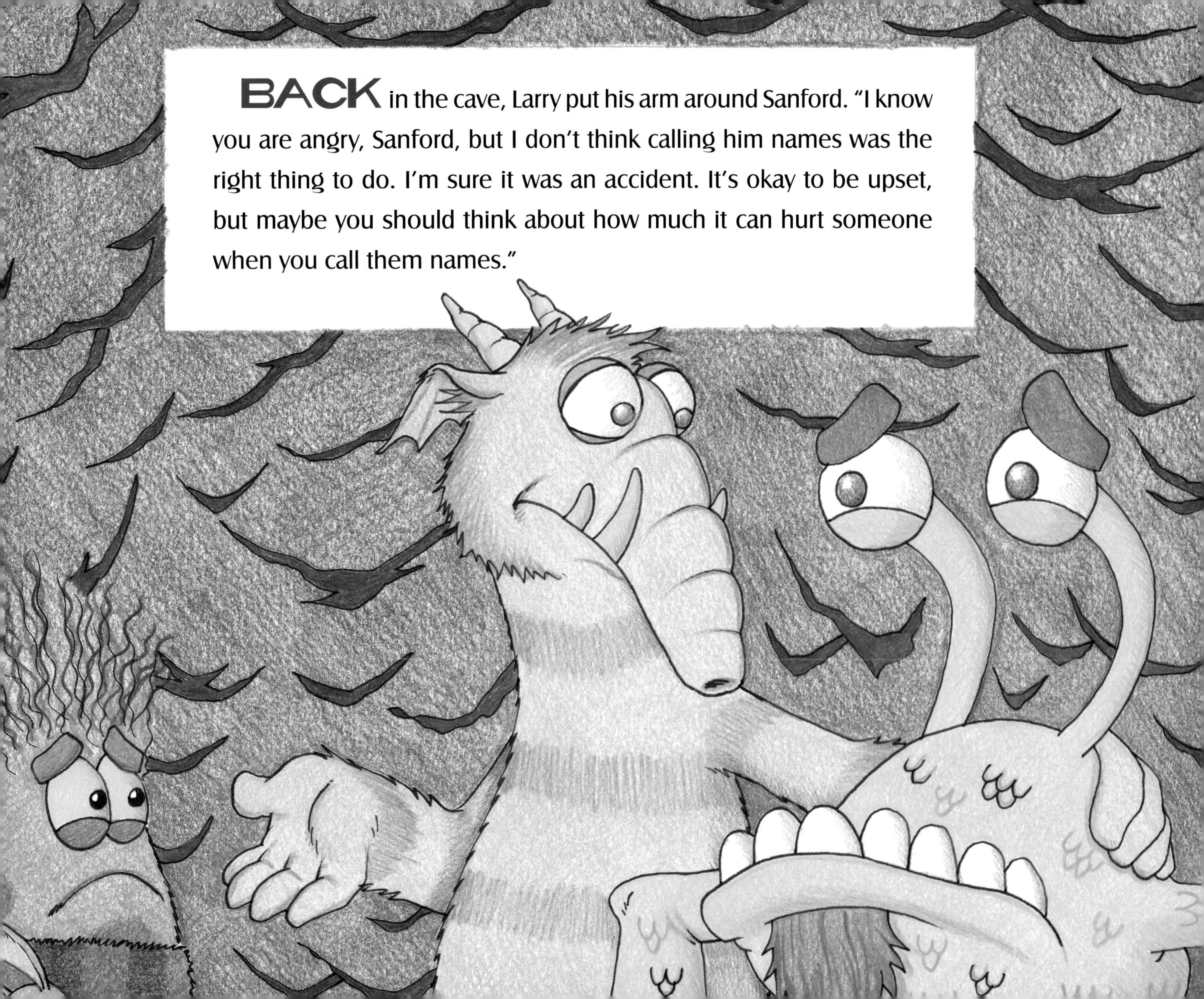

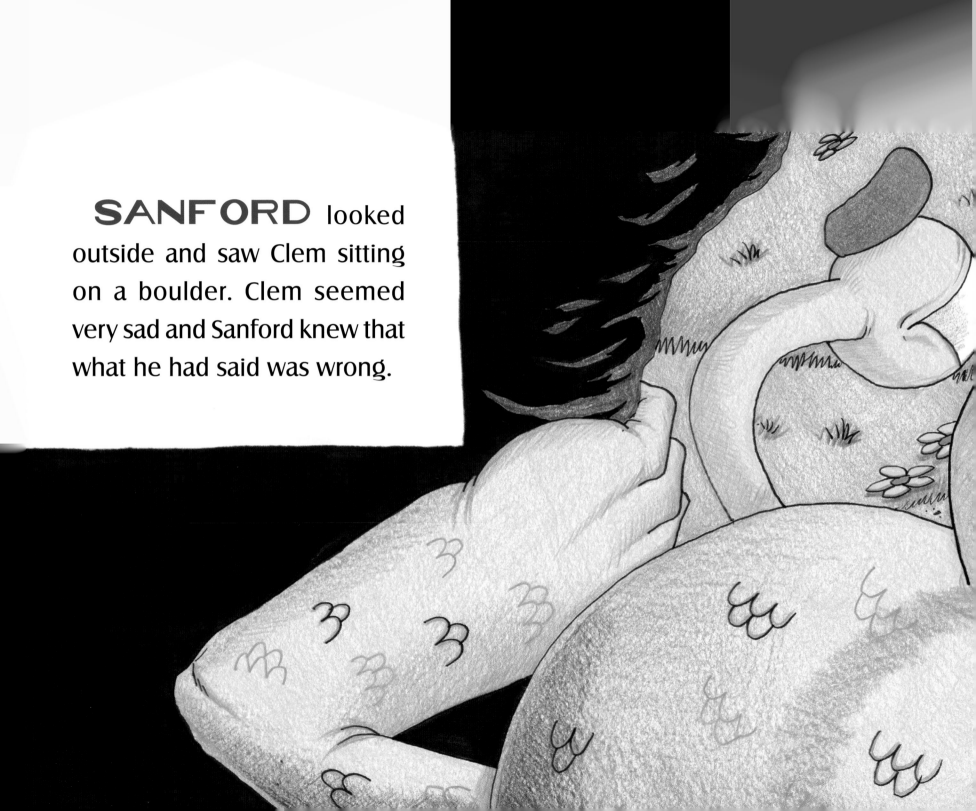

SANFORD looked outside and saw Clem sitting on a boulder. Clem seemed very sad and Sanford knew that what he had said was wrong.

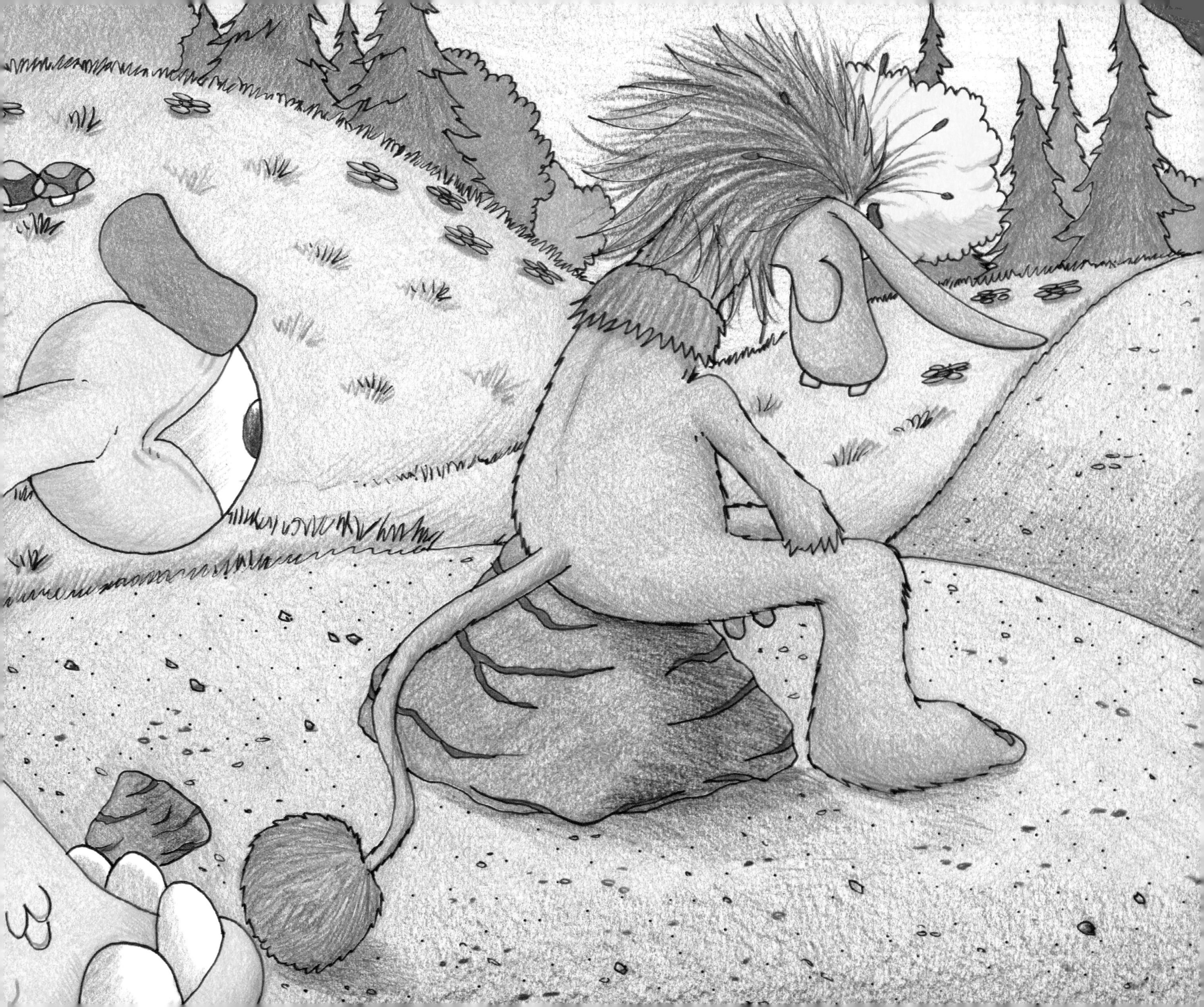

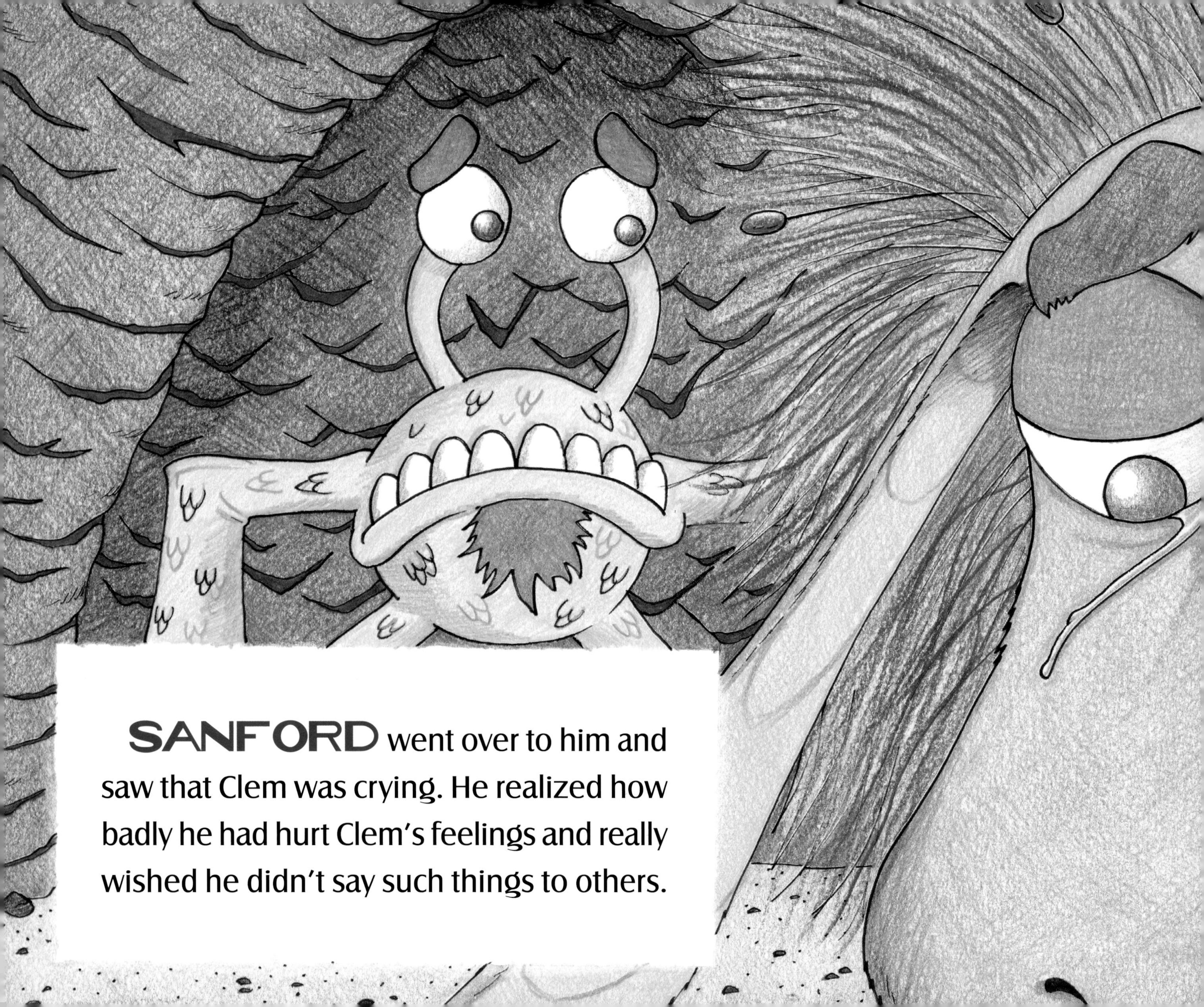

SANFORD went over to him and saw that Clem was crying. He realized how badly he had hurt Clem's feelings and really wished he didn't say such things to others.

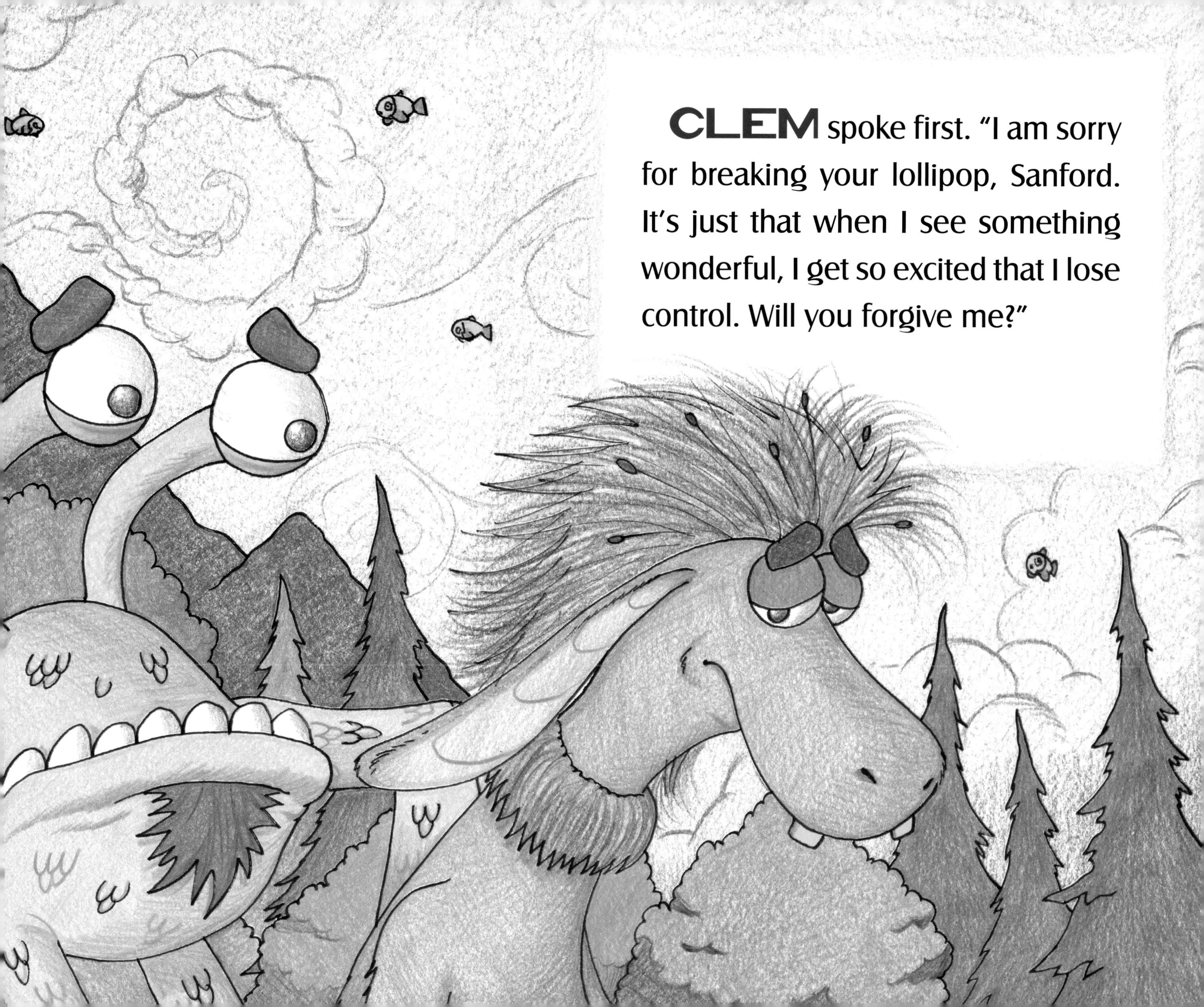

CLEM spoke first. "I am sorry for breaking your lollipop, Sanford. It's just that when I see something wonderful, I get so excited that I lose control. Will you forgive me?"

"OF course I forgive you and… I'm sorry too, Clem." Sanford said. "It was an accident and calling you names was not the right thing to do. I didn't mean it, just like I know you didn't mean to break the lollipop."

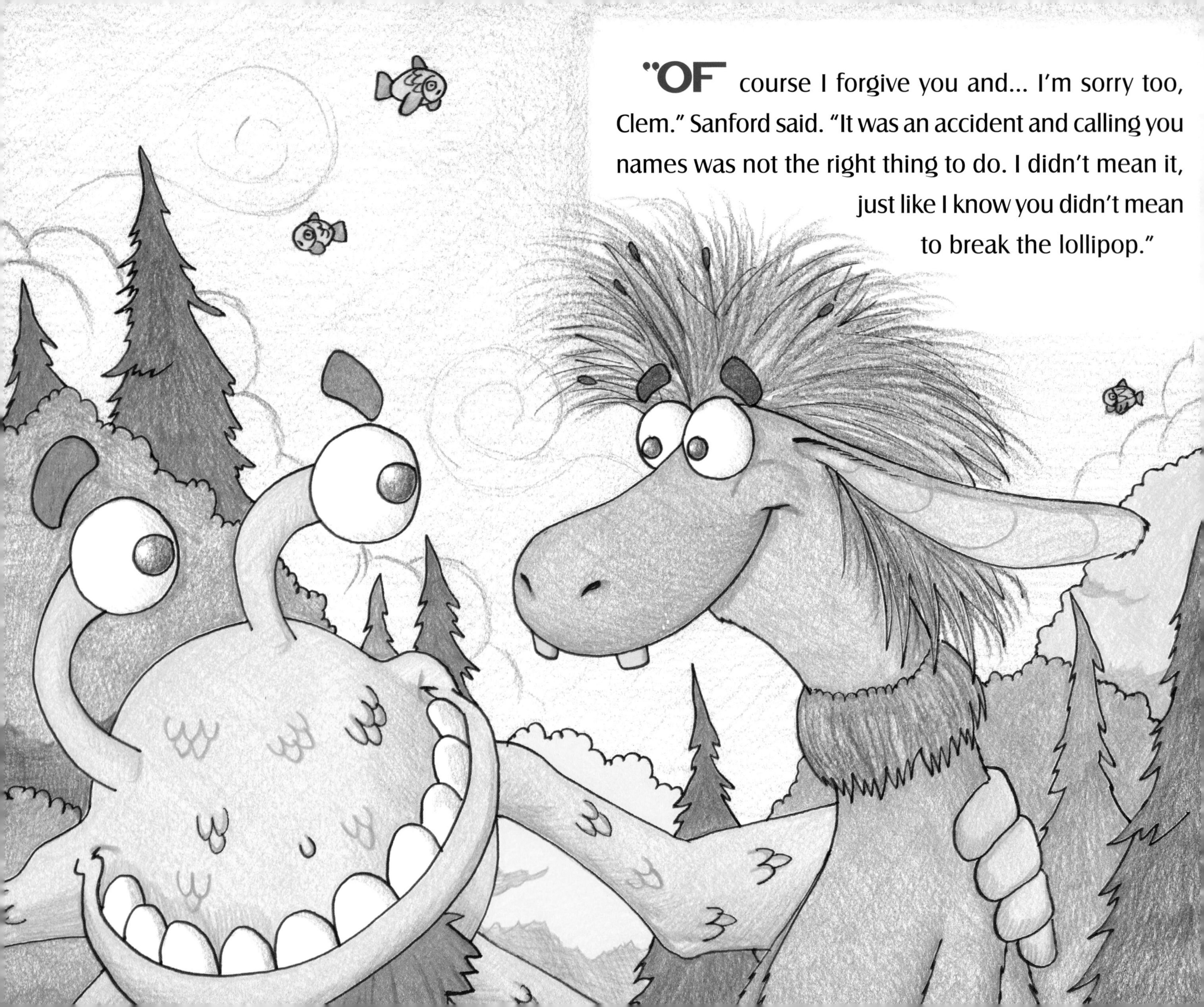

"**BESIDES**, I got something even better for my birthday…I got a new friend!" Sanford stated.

"Wow! Three new friends in one day!" Clem said.

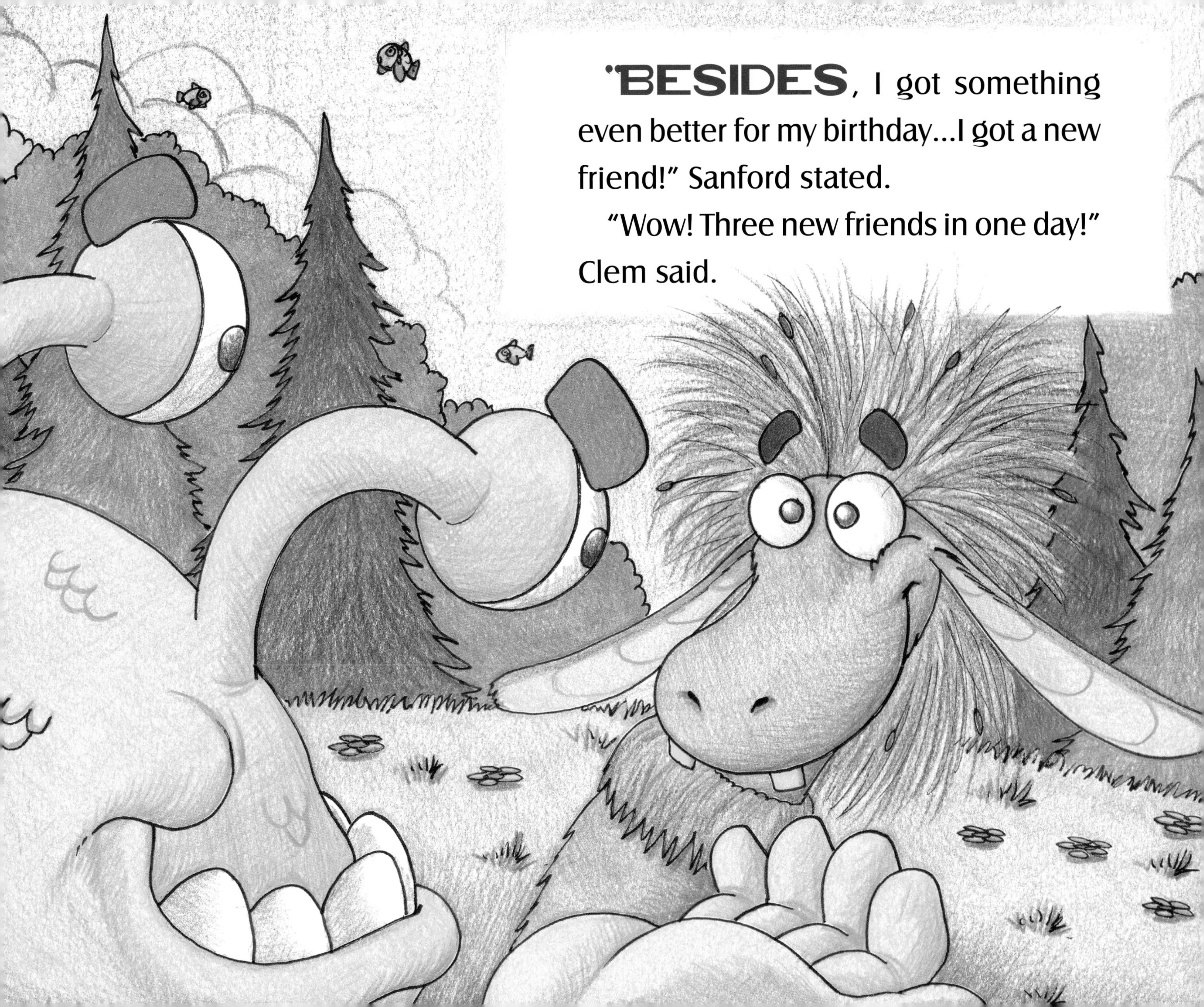

HE could feel himself getting excited again, but this time he tried very hard to keep his feelings under control. So, when Sanford said "Let's shake on it, Buddy!" Clem was very happy and shook Sanford's hand for a long time.

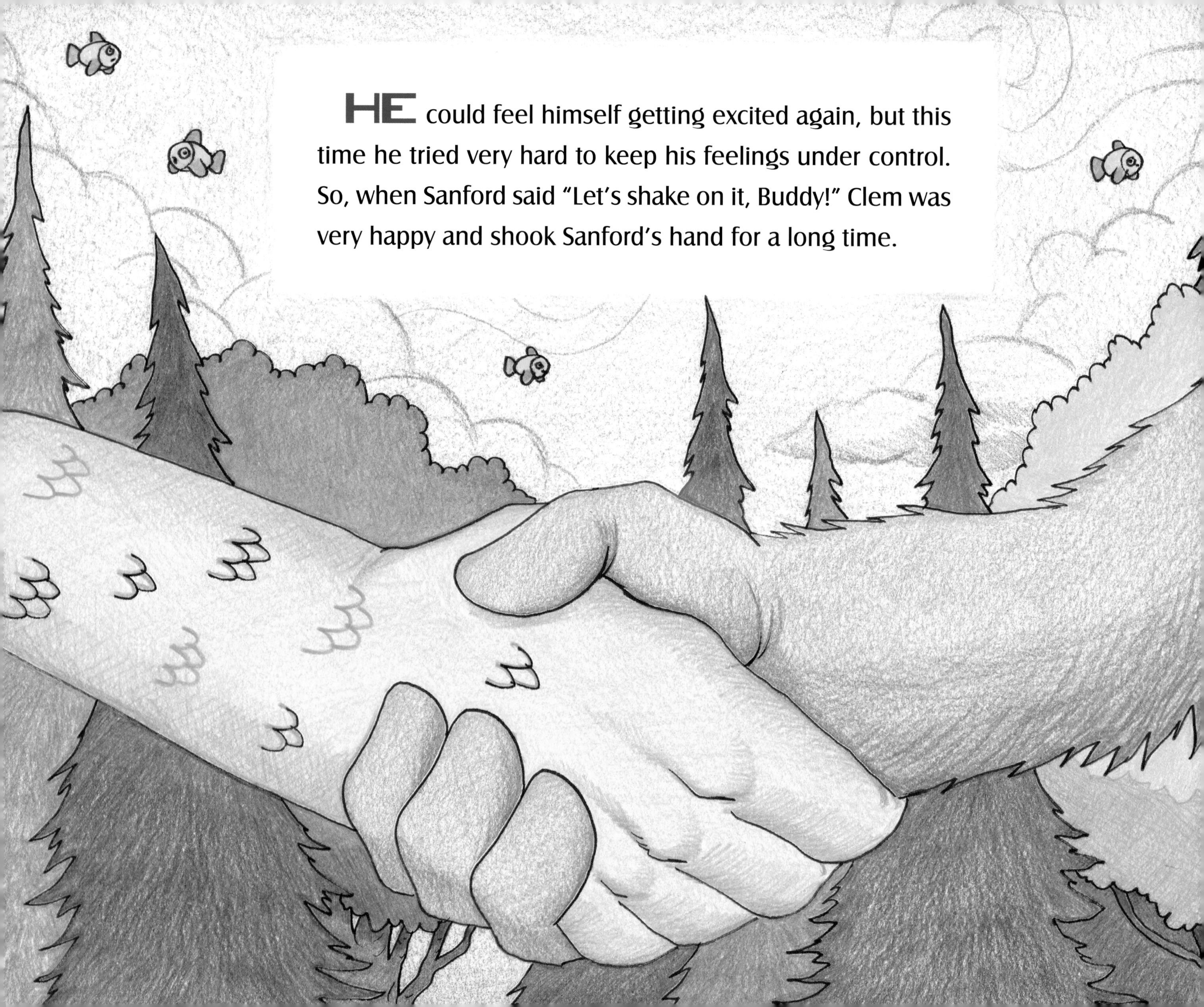

AS the two new friends walked back to the cave, Clem waved at Zabby and Larry. "We're back!" said Sanford with a great big smile.

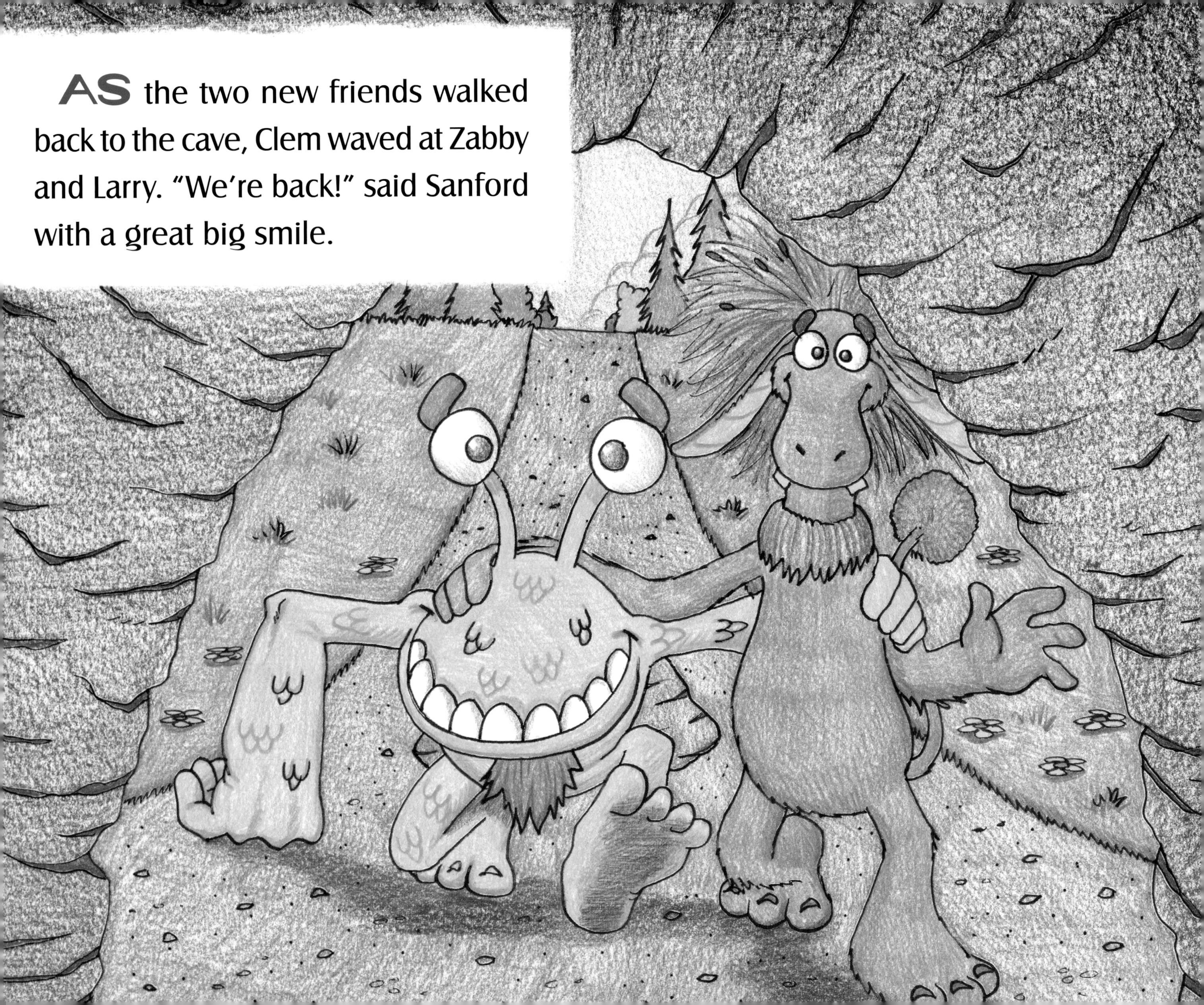

"SO, is everything all right between you two?" Zabby asked.

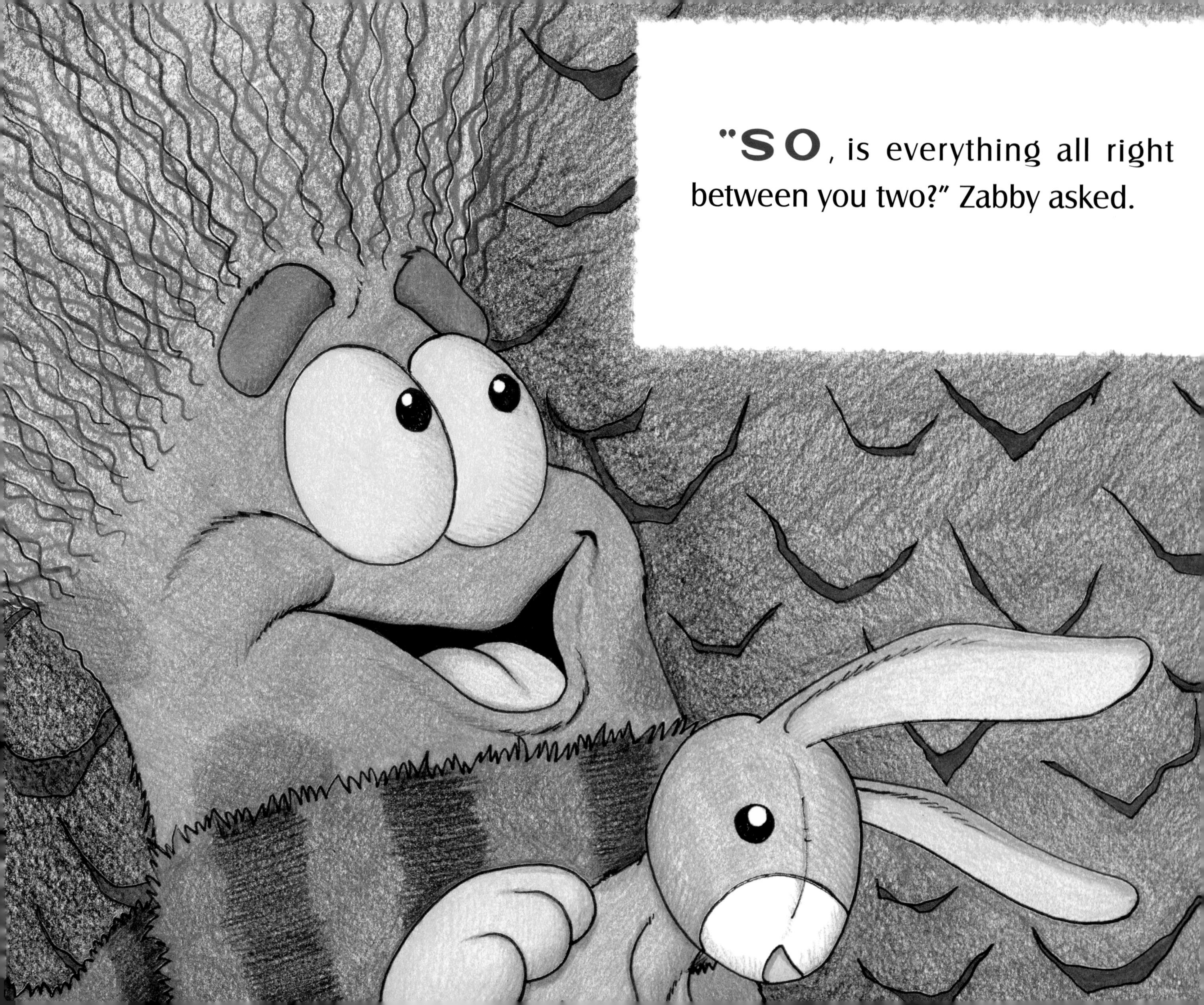

"**WELL**, lollipops don't last forever, but friendships do," said Sanford, "Thanks for a great birthday everyone!"

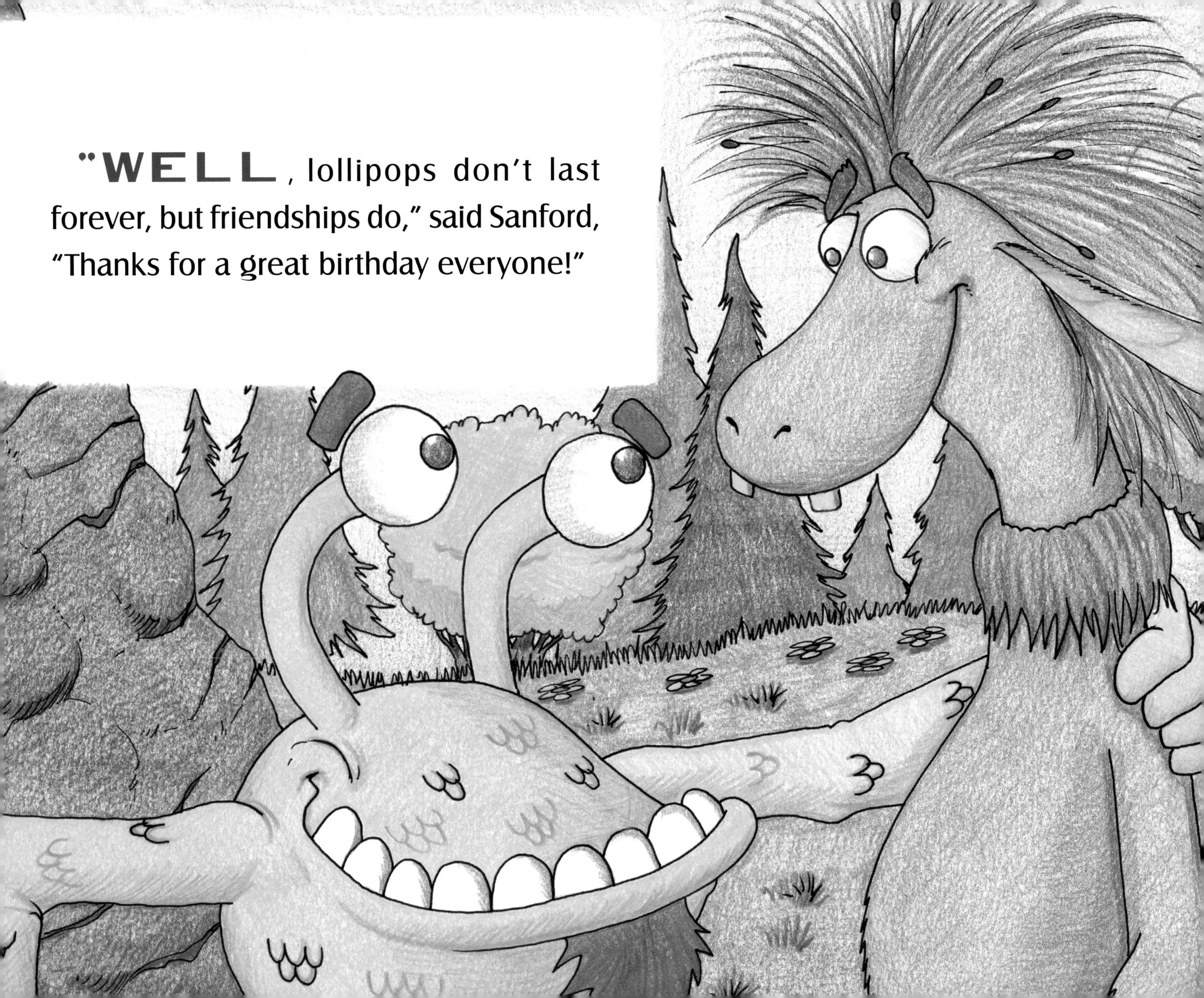

ZABBY and Larry were very happy with the way Sanford and Clem handled their differences, and they gave each other the thumbs-up sign to show their approval.

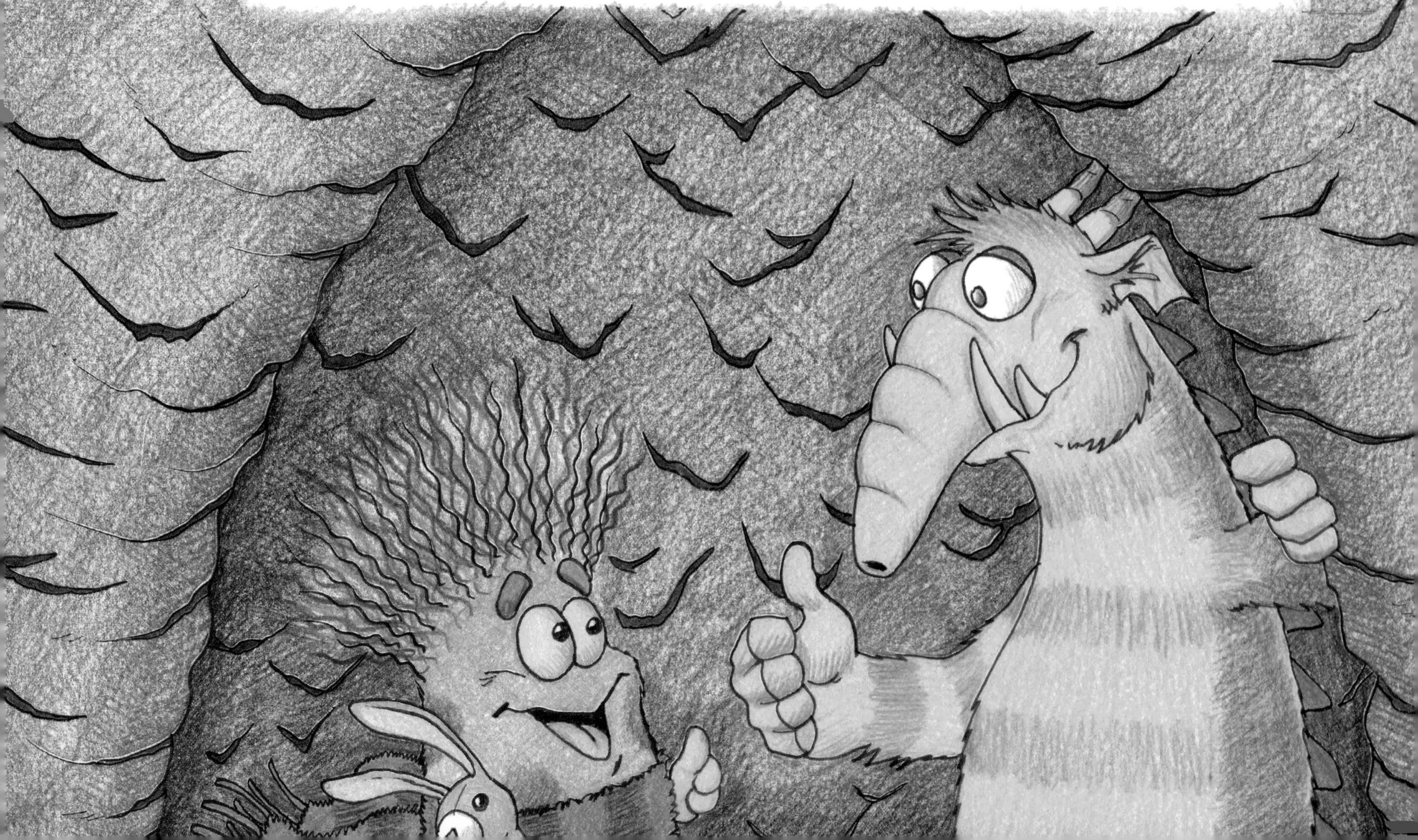

TURNING his brown lollipop bag upside down, Larry said "I would love to celebrate with delicious lollipops, but we're all out."

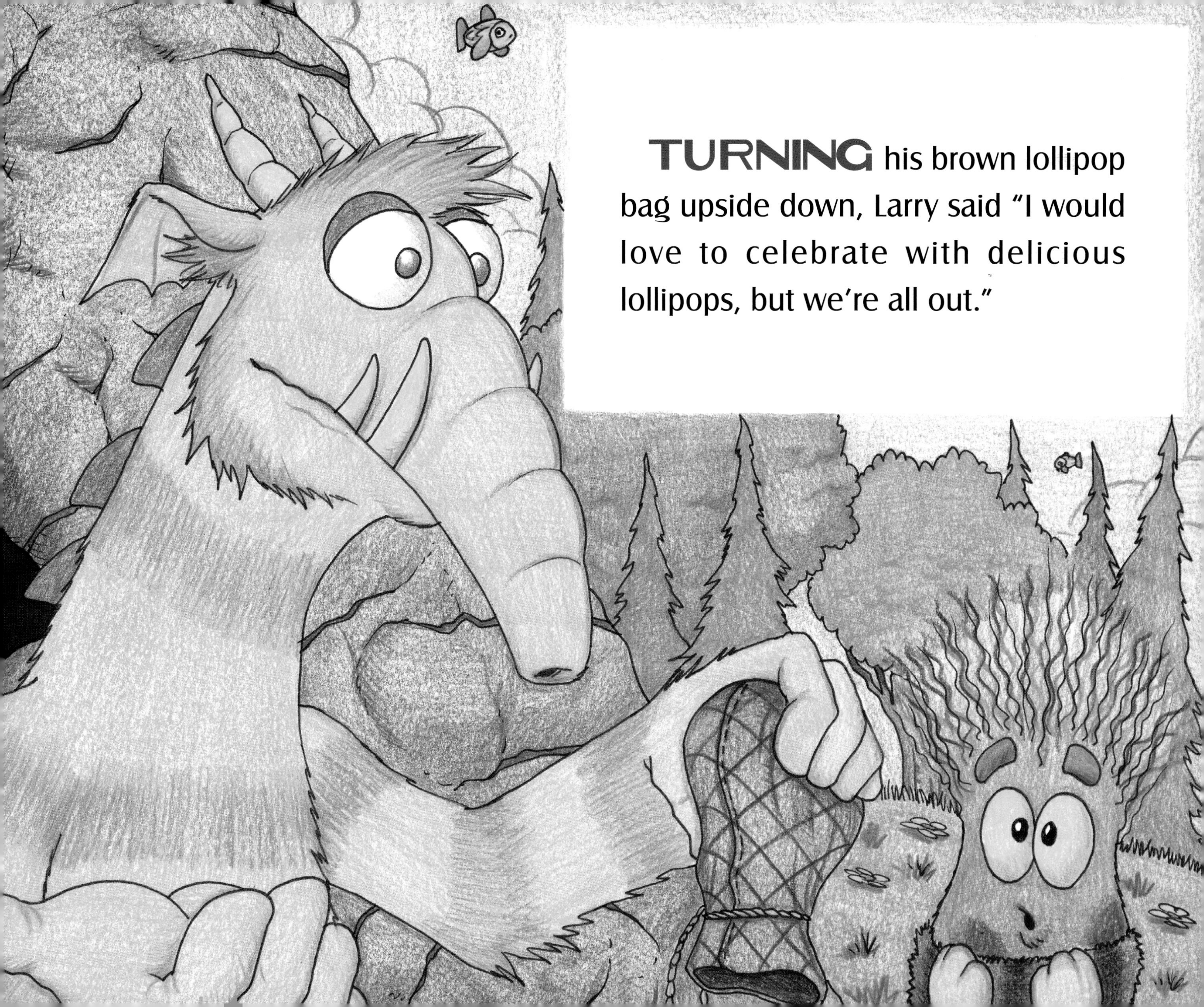

ZABBY thought about this for a moment, then her face lit up! "I have an idea!" she exclaimed. She spun around and quickly ran into the cave.

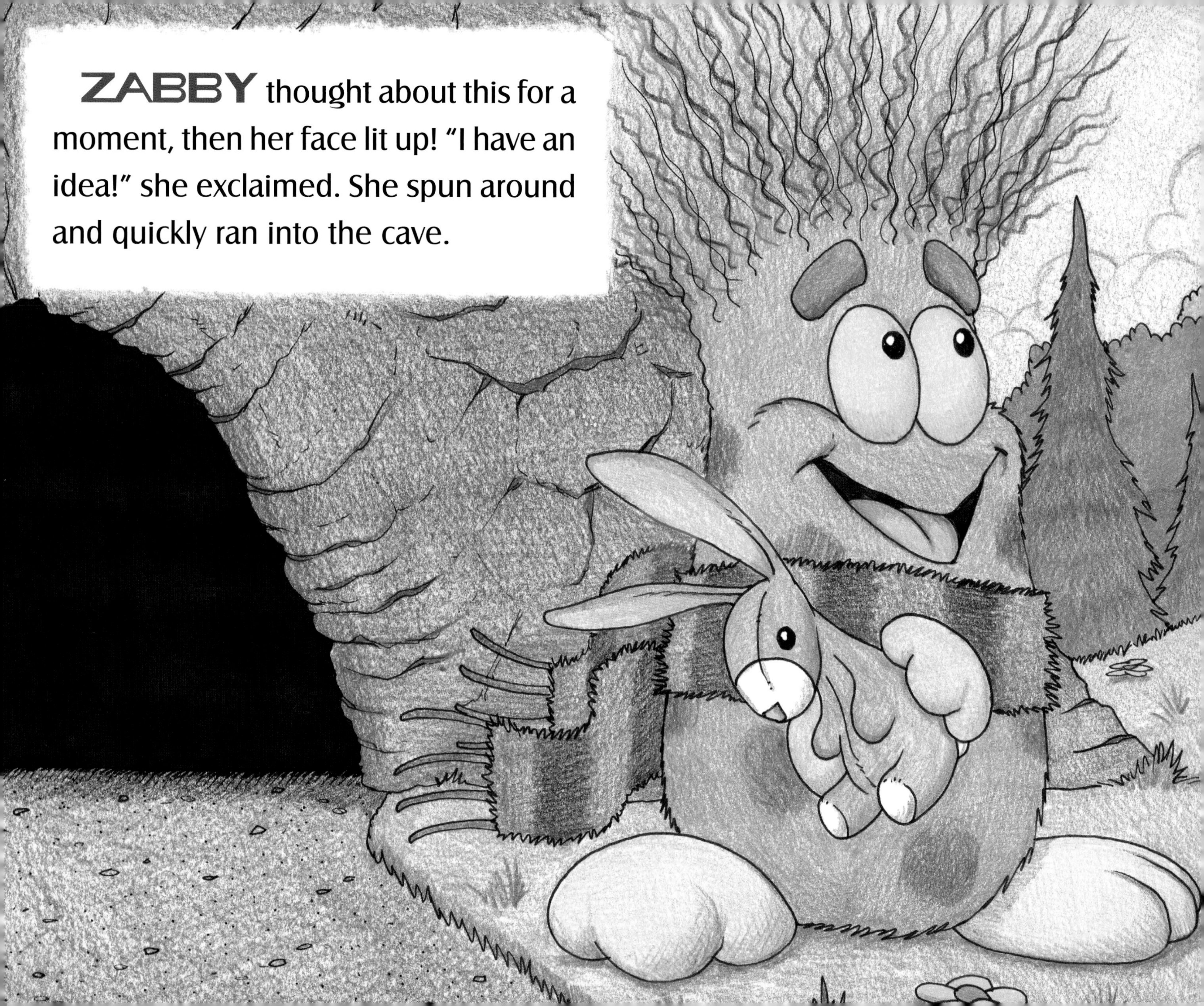

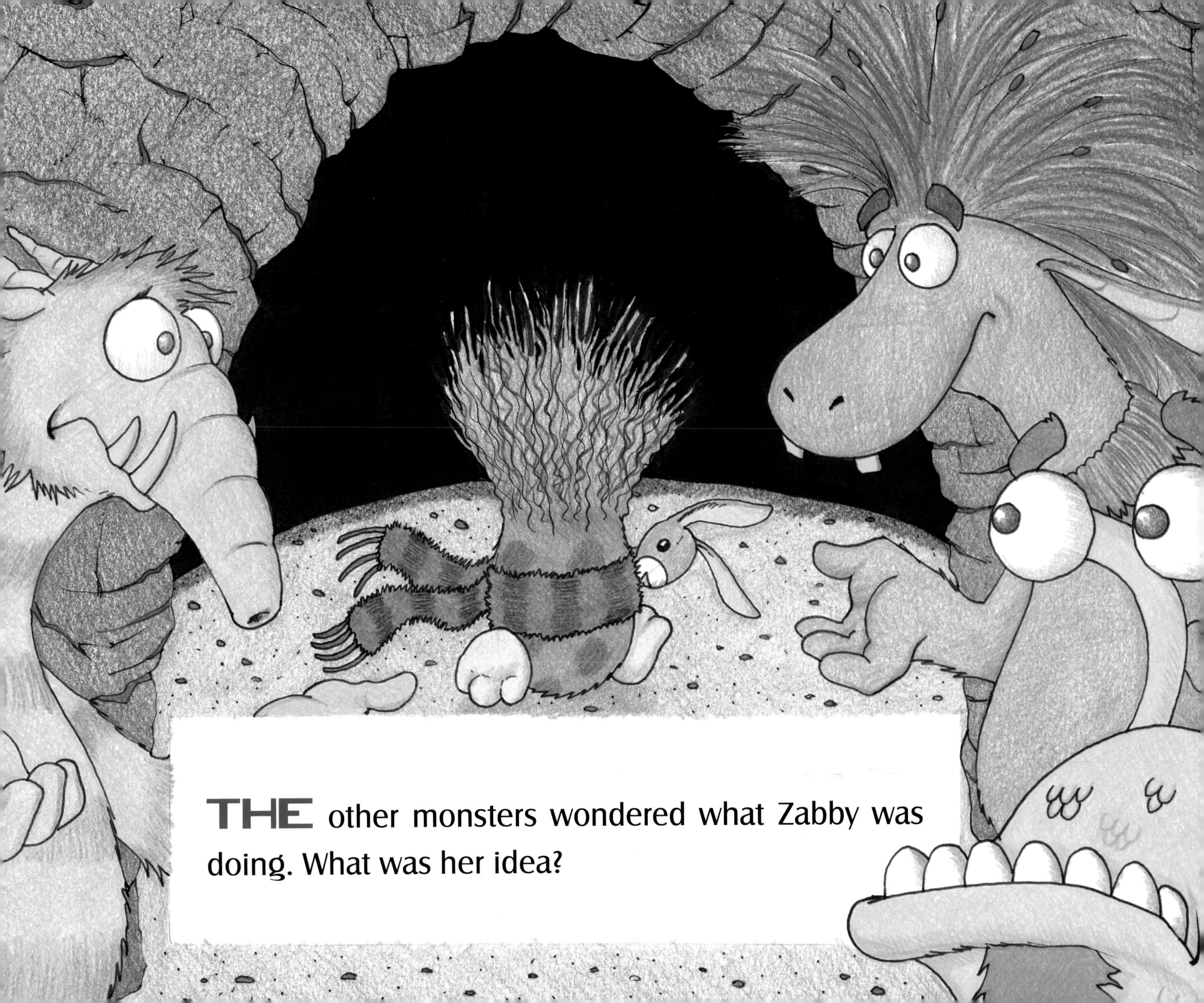

THE other monsters wondered what Zabby was doing. What was her idea?

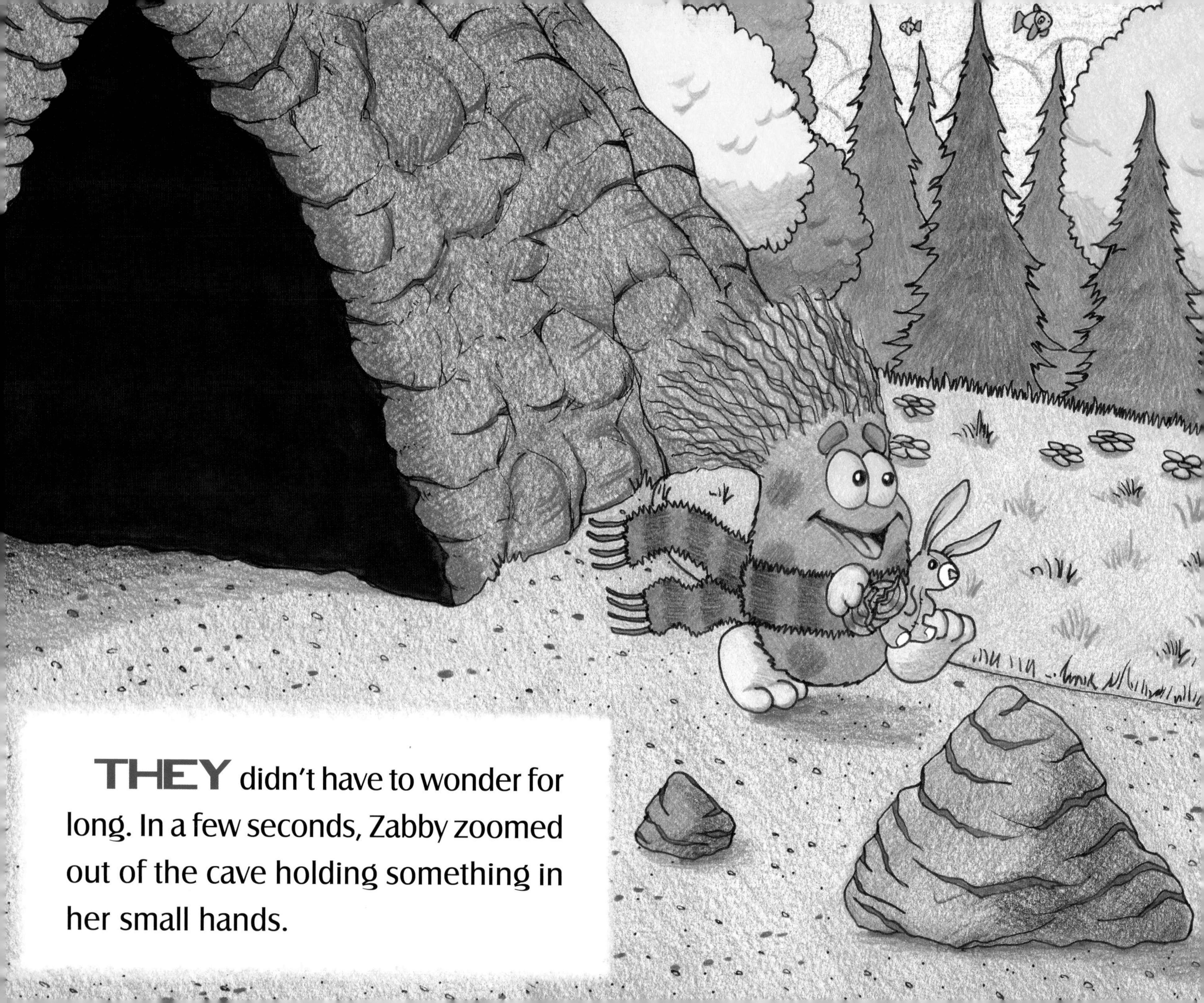

THEY didn't have to wonder for long. In a few seconds, Zabby zoomed out of the cave holding something in her small hands.

AS she approached her friends, they saw that, whatever she was holding, it sparkled in the light.

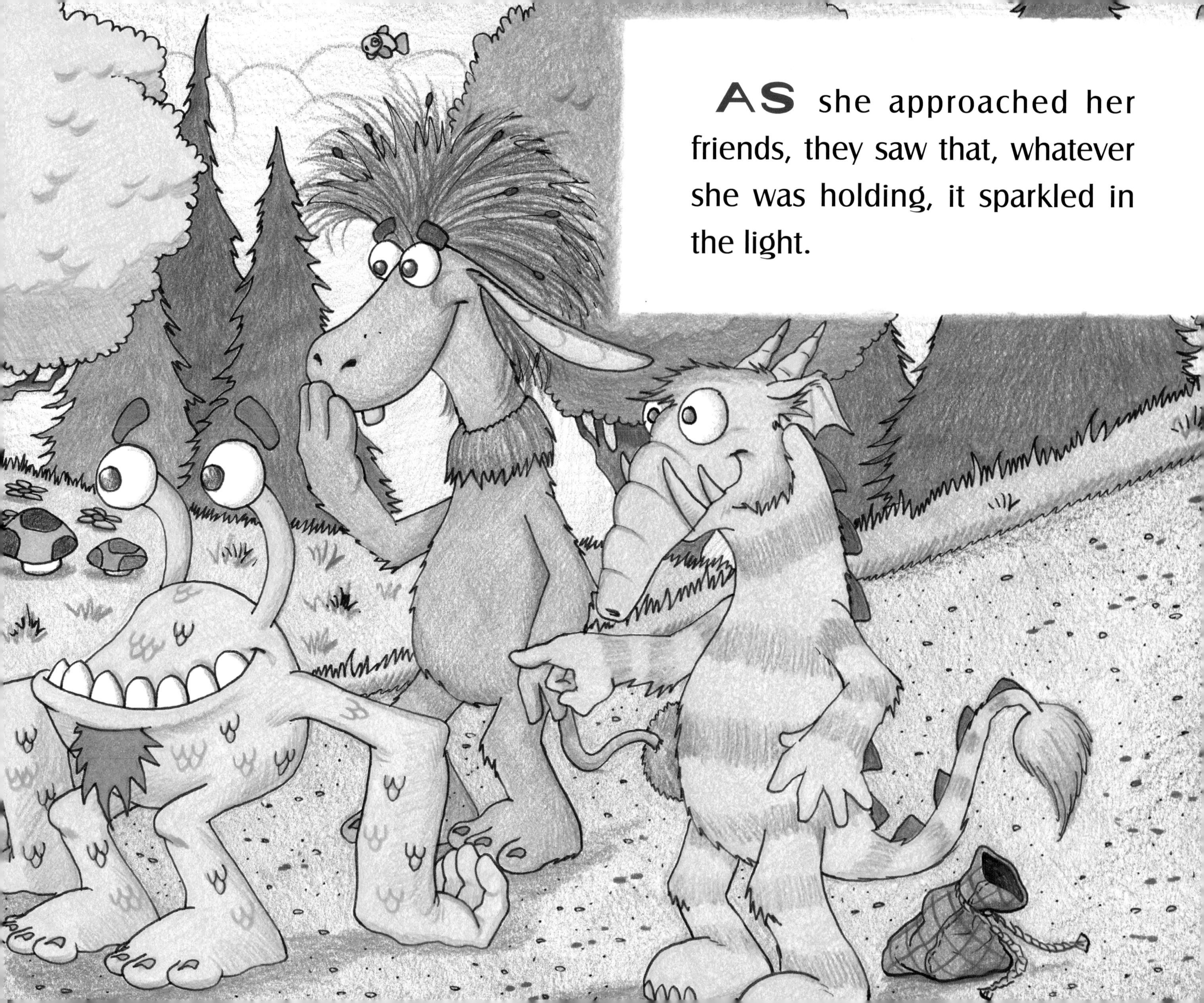

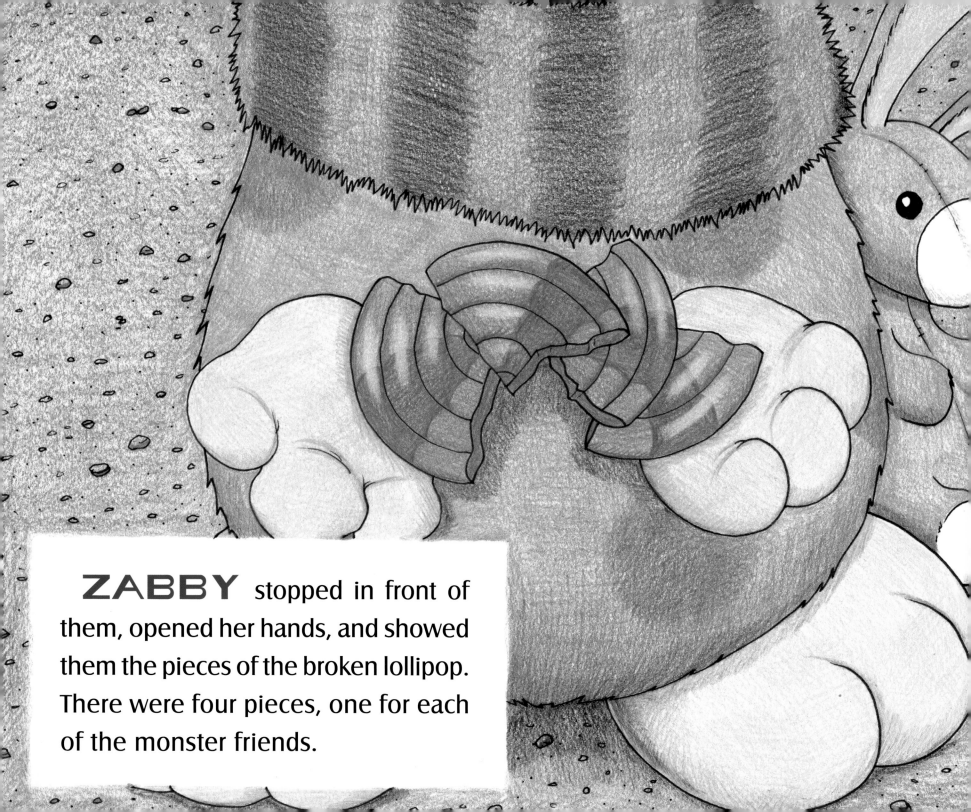

ZABBY stopped in front of them, opened her hands, and showed them the pieces of the broken lollipop. There were four pieces, one for each of the monster friends.

ZABBY'S idea was wonderful! They held the pieces of lollipop up in the air and let out a great cheer. "Great job, Zabby! Now we can all share." said Sanford.

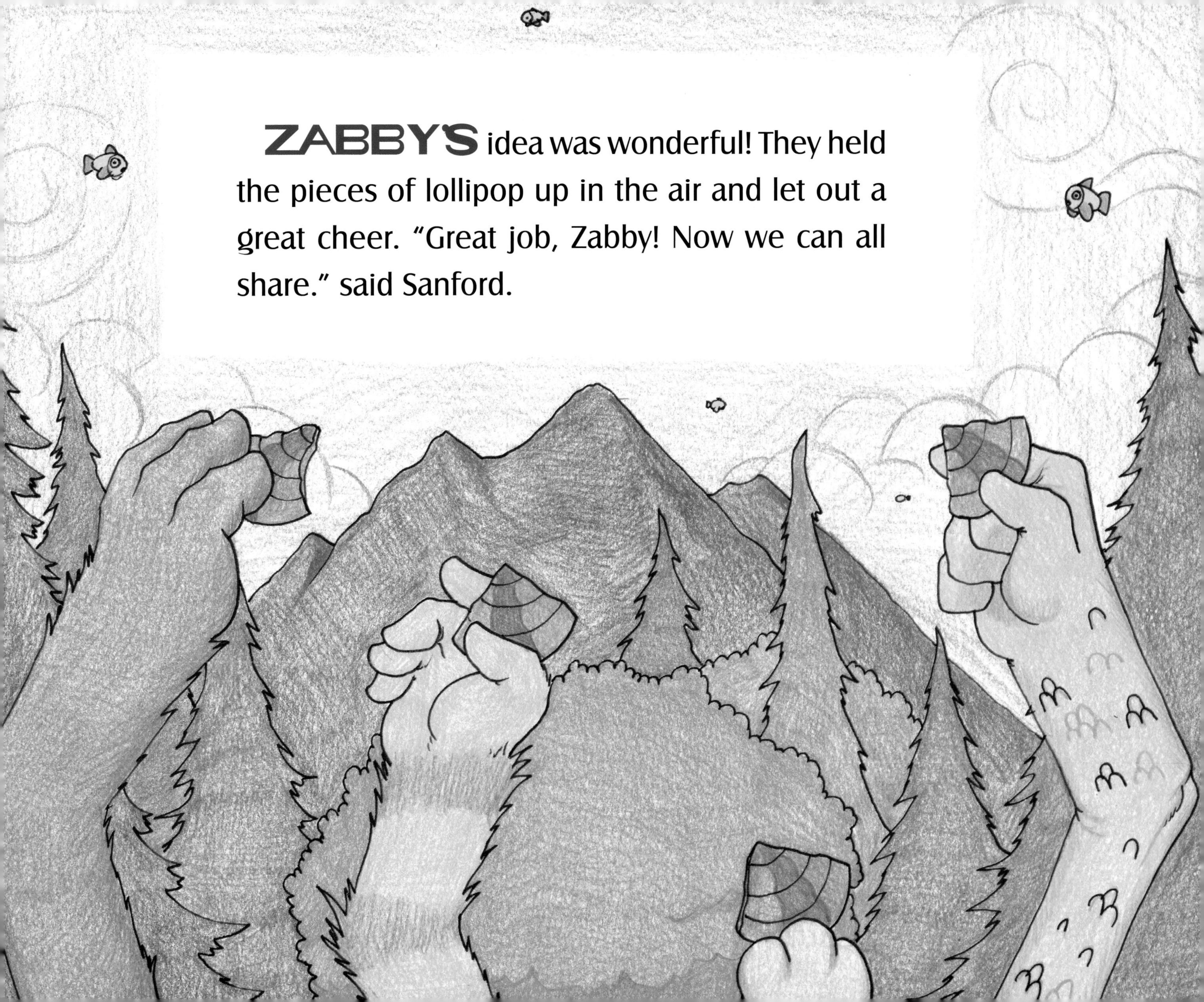

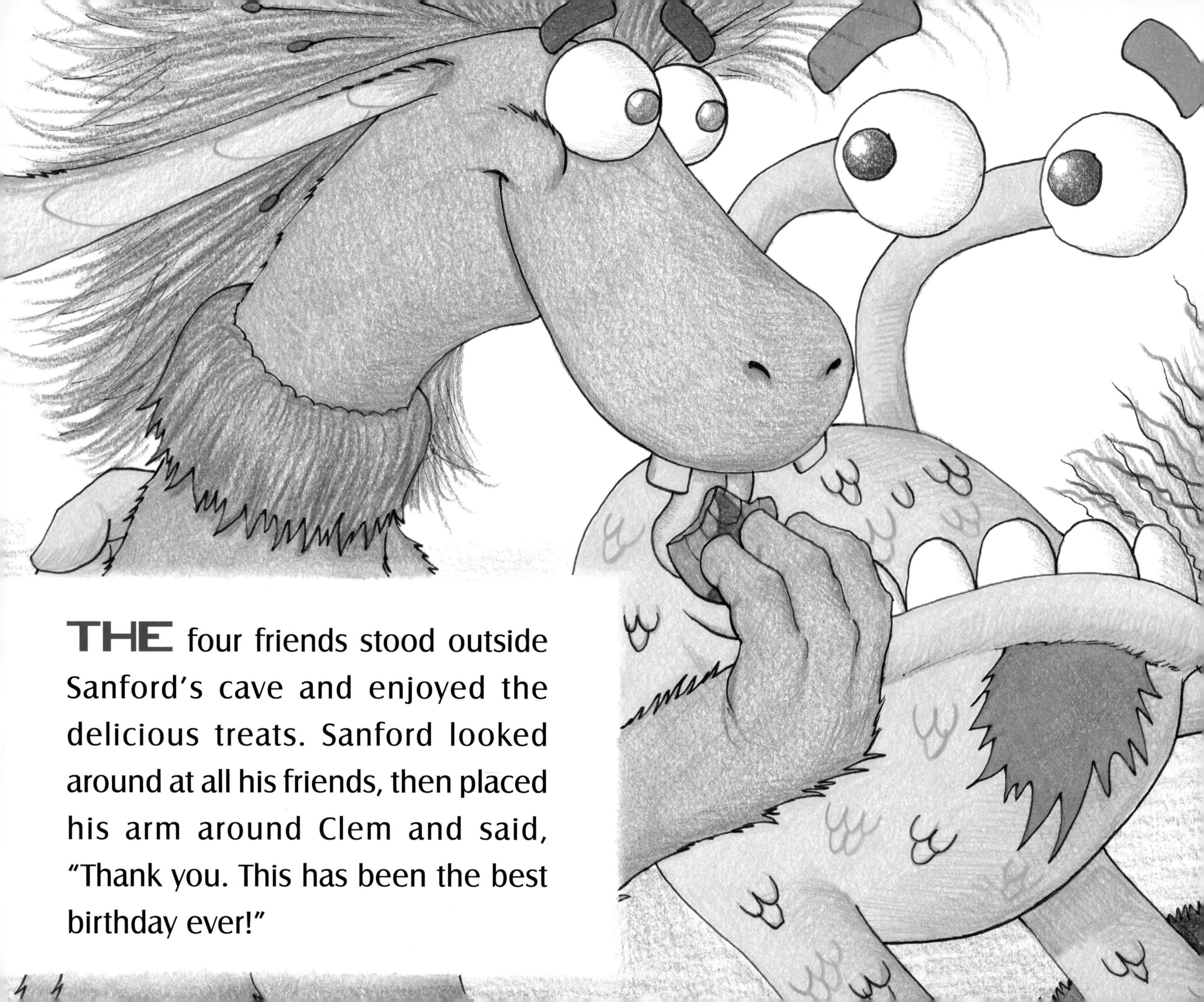

THE four friends stood outside Sanford's cave and enjoyed the delicious treats. Sanford looked around at all his friends, then placed his arm around Clem and said, "Thank you. This has been the best birthday ever!"